THIRTEEN-*Year* CRUSH

THIRTEEN-*Year* CRUSH

JESS JEFFERIES

Just Add Ink Publishing

For Chris, my forever person.

Thank you for making me laugh when I feel like crying and being my calm and safe space. I love you!

ACKNOWLEDGMENTS

This book was so much fun to write. I have my fair share of fantasy works that I've started. But when I had the idea for a romance story, I just had to get the words out. Ever since I was a little girl, I've wanted to write a book. As I got older there were so many things happening, like marriage, kids, and work, that the timing never seemed right.

So first, I'd like to thank my wonderful husband, Chris, who has always encouraged me, has never hesitated at my crazy ideas, and has not only given me three amazing kids but also the strength to follow my dreams. Thank you, Chris, for always being there for me, answering all my random questions, and listening to my different plots and story ideas.

Thank you to Melody Jeffries, a talented book cover designer and great friend. I love how you took all the random bits and pieces of information and created the most magnificent cover that truly brings Holly and Greg to life.

Thank you to Breanna, Christina, and the team at Ever Editing. This being my debut novel as a self-publisher, there was so much for me to learn. I appreciate your patience and guidance as I learn all that goes into getting my story ready for the world.

To my friends, thank you for your patience and support as I talked your ear off about all things self-publishing and story related. You all are amazing and I am so thankful to have each of you in my life. You are more than just friends to me; you are family.

To my family and kids, thank you for helping mold me into the mom, daughter, wife, sister, aunt, niece, and cousin that I am today. You all are a never-ending stream of encouragement and love. Love you!

Lastly, to my readers, thank you for taking a chance on a new author. You are making my dreams come true!

THIRTEEN-*Year* CRUSH

PROLOGUE
Greg

Before I have a chance to register what I'm doing, I scramble to my feet, desperate to move Holly out of the way. The baseball-helmet bowl I'm holding dumps popcorn everywhere as I quickly jump forward. My soda lands on Trent, soaking his pants. "Hey!" he yells, but I'm not thinking about any of that. I just know I have to act fast. I don't want Holly to get hurt.

My arm shoots out, and I push Holly to the side just in time.

Two hours earlier . . .

By the time I find my lower-level outfield seat in the stadium, I'm jittery, full of excitement for the upcoming game.

Under normal circumstances, I wouldn't have made it to this baseball game. However, these are not normal circumstances. I have a good reason to be here: Holly.

When my middle school offered any kid who reached the top reading goal a trip to a Sounds Minor League Baseball game, I knew without a doubt that my sister, Gwen, and her best friend, Holly Palmer, would be there. And knowing that Holly would be there, I had to earn my spot too. After roping in my best friend, Trent, we read the heck out of the *Everworld* and *Goosebumps* series and made the cut for the game.

Now Holly and Gwen are sitting right in front of Trent and me. Trent pulls a piece of popcorn out of my baseball-helmet bowl.

"What are you doing?" I ask.

"Watch this," he says, throwing the kernel at Gwen.

She doesn't notice, so he sends another, and then a handful.

"Hey!" says Gwen, whipping around. "What do you all think you're doing?"

Trent shrugs. "I don't know what you're talking about."

"It wasn't us," I say, backing him up.

When Gwen turns around, Trent throws another piece, this time at Holly. The kernel catches at the bottom of her brown hair.

Her hair shimmers from the sunlight. Soft curls bounce as she talks to Gwen about the game. I can't help watching her. Her smile. Her lips. The ways she brushes her hair away from her face, causing the popcorn kernel to sway but not fall.

I lean over to get the popcorn out. And when my fingers touch the end of her sunlit hair, it's just as soft as I imagined.

"I saw that!" says Gwen, smacking my hand. "Greg, leave us alone."

Holly turns around her, locking her eyes with mine. "Were you throwing popcorn at us, Greg?"

My stomach flip-flops. "I . . . I . . ." I fumble over my words, too distracted to form a sentence.

"Not cool, Greg," Trent teases, elbowing me in the ribs.

"What? No, it wasn't. . . . I mean . . ." I'm too caught up in Holly's gaze. I can't find any words.

But then Holly reaches into her pretzel bites and tosses one, hitting me square on the forehead. She giggles. I reach into my baseball helmet and grab a popcorn kernel, tossing it at her. If I'm going to get blamed, might as well throw some, right?

The kernel bounces off Holly's cheek and lands on Gwen. Gwen tears off a piece of her cotton candy and throws it at me.

"It's on!" says Trent, joining in.

Before we know it, we're throwing popcorn, pretzels, and cotton candy at each other like it's a snowball fight.

"Hey," says one of the chaperones. "Knock that off. You're supposed to be watching the game."

Stifling giggles, the girls turn back around.

Trent nudges my elbow, tilting his head at Holly. "About time you start flirting with her," he says.

I nudge him back harder. "Trent!" I hiss. "She's right there."

"Sorry." He shrugs, and we both turn our attention back to the game.

By the seventh-inning stretch, the Sounds are up by three runs.

The song "I'm Alright" by Jo Dee Messina blasts through the stadium. Gwen jumps up. "I love this song," she says, pulling Holly to her feet. Gwen waves her arms above her head. Holly joins in too, swaying back and forth.

Back and forth.

My attention quickly turns from the baseball game to Holly. I'm mesmerized.

Back and forth.

"Let's join them!" says Trent, jumping up.

Back and forth.

"Greg?" he asks.

Back and forth.

"Greg!"

"What?" I snap out of it, looking over at him in confusion.

"Want to join them?" he asks again.

"No way," I say, keeping my eyes on Holly.

"You're just enjoying the view, aren't you?"

"I . . . it's not what you think."

"Sure," says Trent. A wide grin spreads across his face.

When the song ends, Holly turns around to take her seat. We lock eyes again. Her cheeks are pink from dancing. I have no excuse for looking at her, but she doesn't question it. She gives me a smile before sitting down.

My pulse races.

Glancing over her shoulder, she smiles at me again.

My face reddens.

At the bottom of the ninth, the sun is bright and high in the sky. The Sounds have given up the lead to the Barons and left both teams tied. The Sounds are up to bat. The first two batters strike out, and the third gets a walk.

"Come on!" yells Trent, throwing a fist in the air.

"Go, Sounds!" adds Gwen.

The next batter walks to the plate. The pitcher throws, and *crack!* The batter hits the ball so hard the sound reverberates through the entire stadium. The ball goes high. I, along with the rest of the audience, squint into the sun hoping to get a better view.

Players run around the bases. The Baron outfielders race toward the batter's eye.

I hold my hand above my eyes, trying to block out the bright sun.

Suddenly, there it is.

The ball looks like it's heading for the stands. It gets closer and closer, heading right toward our school's area. Right toward Holly.

I jump to my feet, dropping my soda and dumping the remaining popcorn from my baseball helmet. "Watch out!" I yell. I dive in between Holly and Gwen, shoving them to the side.

I land on the armrest between them. Holly falls to the floor, and Gwen stumbles over the girl sitting next to her.

The baseball lands smack dab in the baseball-helmet bowl I am still holding. I quickly slap my hand over the baseball, hoping to stop it from popping back out.

"Are you okay, Palmer?" I ask Holly, slowly getting to my feet.

"Yeah," she says. "Are you?"

My hand burns and my side hurts from landing on the arm of the seat. "I . . . I think so." I lean over and offer Holly my hand. When she takes it, a jolt runs up my arm. "It looked like it was heading straight for you," I say, wrapping my fingers around hers.

"I know." She wraps hers fingers around mine. "Thanks for catching it."

"I couldn't let it hit you." I smile.

She smiles back, looking into my eyes, the baseball-helmet bowl—still holding the ball—placed snuggly between us.

"Dude, I can't believe you caught that!" Trent slaps me on the back, loosening my hold on Holly's hand. "Even if you did spill your soda all over me."

"Hellooo!" whines Gwen, still sprawled on the ground. "What about me?"

"Oh, Gwen," Holly says, dropping my hand. "Are you okay?"

Suddenly I'm swarmed by middle schoolers whooping and hollering. I'm grinning from ear to ear.

After the game, our group is invited to meet the baseball players. I get a lot of attention for catching the final home run ball. The player who hit the ball even signs it for me. Which is really cool. Almost as cool as holding Holly's hand for the first time.

As we leave the stadium to head back to the buses, I call out to Holly. "Palmer, wait up."

She glances around before catching my eye in the crowd.

When I finally maneuver my way next to her, I hold out the baseball. "I believe this is rightfully yours."

"But you caught it," she says, meeting my eyes.

"I . . . I know, but it . . . it was heading to you." Trying to give her the ball, I take her hand in mine. My fingers tingle at the touch. "So, it should be yours, right?"

"But I didn't notice it," she says. "You shoved me out of the way just in time."

"It wasn't a big deal."

"Yes, it was." She drops my hand before wrapping both her arms around me.

I feel my heart racing. Is this what it feels like to have a heart attack? I'm too young for that. Right? How is it even possible for her to make me feel this way?

"Thanks, Greg," she whispers.

I feel light and heavy at the same time. I feel happy and terrified. I want to hug her back, but my stomach is doing so many flip-flops that I think I might throw up. And that's the last thing I want to do in front of Holly. I have to get out of here, and fast.

I pull back from her hug and drop the ball in her hand. "Keep it," I say. And then I hightail it out of there.

THIRTEEN YEARS

Later . . . .

CHAPTER 1
Holly

"Holly, please come to the cabin with us," Gwen pleads over the phone. "It's been ages since we've been on a trip together. You need to get out and have some fun, and I need my best friend! And you haven't been to the cabin in years!"

I bite my lip. "I don't know. . . ."

"Come on, Greg and Trent will be there too. It will be fun! You know you want to."

"It's just that I'm not sure that Maverick would be okay with it," I reply.

"Not to be mean, but I don't care if Maverick is okay with it or not."

"I know you two haven't always gotten along, but as his girlfriend, I do care what he thinks."

"Would he even realize you were gone?" Gwen asks.

"Of course he would!"

"I didn't mean it like that," Gwen says and sighs. "It's just that he's so caught up in his own life."

Not wanting to dwell on this topic, I ask, "What days were you saying it was again?"

"This weekend, all of next week, and through the next weekend."

I scroll through the calendar on my phone. "You know what?" I tell Gwen. "It looks like Maverick has a work trip and will be out of town that week."

"Perfect! You should totally come."

"I'll run it by him and see."

"Run it by him? What maniac would tell you to stay behind while he isn't even there?" Gwen presses.

"It's not like that, and you know it."

"Actually, I don't know that I do. I've never thought you two were a good match."

I let out a sigh and change the subject again. "Could we fly up together?"

"Well, see here's the thing. I'm actually not home right now. I'm in LA."

"Why are you in LA?"

"There was a huge event-planner convention, one of the biggest of the year. I couldn't pass up the opportunity to network and get some great new ideas, so I flew out for it."

"That sounds great for your business," I say.

"It has been amazing. I really have gotten some great ideas that I can't wait to try out . . . after our trip to the cabin."

"Okay, okay, I get it. Let me look up some flights. No promises though."

Putting down my cocoa and opening my laptop, I skim the list for flights from Nashville, Tennessee, to Rutland, Vermont. "Looks like the earliest I could get is a 1:00 p.m. flight tomorrow, so after the drive to the cabin, I'm looking at getting there tomorrow night. When would you fly in, G?"

"I don't get in until the day after, but it's early, like 9:00 a.m."

"Okay, that's pretty good. What about the boys?"

"Greg is supposed to fly in from his place in New York just after I'm supposed to land, and Trent is flying in later that night. He wanted to come earlier, but he's got some event happening at the marina that he has to oversee."

"Okay," I say, tapping my fingers on my desk. At least I wouldn't be alone with Greg or Trent. Maybe Maverick wouldn't mind me going after all, since I wouldn't be having any one-on-one time with the boys. But that also means I would have to make the long drive from the airport to the cabin alone. "Ugh, but that drive by myself sounds awful."

"Why don't you get a car service?" says Gwen. "It could pick you up at the airport and drive you to the lodge."

"I don't know."

"I do it all the time!" says Gwen. "Here, I'm sending you the information for the car service I use right now."

"You sure you'll be the next one to get there after me?" I ask, clicking on the link that just popped up on my phone.

"Yes, I'm sure," says Gwen. "Why?"

"Um, nothing. Don't worry about it," I say, not wanting to bring up Maverick again. "There's nothing wrong with a short trip with my best friend, right?"

"Of course not!"

I twirl a strand of hair around my fingers. "And while I'm waiting for you all, I could work on an article I need to finish up."

"That's a great perk of being a work-from-home journalist," says Gwen.

"It really is."

"Plus, you're going to be so tired when you get there and finish the article that you'll fall right asleep, and when you wake up, I'll be there."

"It does sound like I could pull it off."

"You definitely could! Please Hol, please, please, please. We haven't had a getaway in years."

She's right. The last time we had a vacation together, it had been the summer before I met Maverick. I sigh again, "Okay, but what do I pack?"

Gwen squeals so shrilly that I hold my phone an arm's length away.

I'm adding my favorite hoodie to one of my suitcases when keys jingle in the door. I pause the *Gilmore Girls* episode I'm watching and turn to see Maverick walk in.

"Hi, babe," I say. "I didn't expect to see you tonight."

"So?" he says, stepping into the living room and browsing the books on my bookshelf, sliding some out of their spots. He does this a few times before moving to the baseball I keep on the second shelf. Maverick tosses it lightly in the air and catches it again and again.

"Please don't," I say, walking over to him.

"Why do you even have this old thing?" Maverick asks, holding the ball just out of my reach. "There's nothing special about it. The signature isn't even a famous ballplayer's."

"I just do. I've had it since I was younger."

"You should just throw it out. No sense in keeping these worthless things taking up space," he says, gesturing to my other keepsakes on the shelf. He tosses the ball to me and I catch it, almost tripping over my suitcase in the process.

Once the ball is safely back on my bookshelf, I breathe easier. I take in my other mementos. A huge shell from a trip to the beach with my sisters, a snow globe from a trip Gwen and I took in high school, a Luna Lovegood wand from my first trip to Universal Studios—little knick-knacks that each hold their own memories. I'm not sure what significance the baseball holds for me, probably just the friendships I've had since childhood. But even though I have a few other items that represent those bonds, I can't let this baseball go. Was there something about that Sounds game that I wanted to hold on to?

"So," Maverick says again, "why didn't you expect to see me tonight?"

"Oh, no, I'm so glad you showed up. You know you're welcome anytime. I just—since giving you the key, I thought you might still text me or . . ."

He looks at my suitcases and clothes strewn across the room. "Are you going somewhere?" he asks.

"Oh, well, Gwen's asked me to join her for a little friend's trip."

"Who's going to be there?"

"Well, just the regular gang. Gwen, Trent, Greg, and me."

"No."

"No?"

"No, you will not be going. I don't like you being around those men. I'll be out of town and can't join you. So, it'll have to wait."

"Oh, I mean, I wouldn't have to hang out with Greg or Trent. I was really just hoping for some time with Gwen. We haven't gone on a trip together in ages."

Maverick walks over to me, slipping an arm around my back and tilting my chin up. He kisses me then meets my eyes. "I'm sorry, Sweetie. When I get back from my work trip, we can plan a time to get together with Gwen and the others if that's what you'd like."

"But I'm not sure if that will work out with everyone else's schedules and the cabin we're planning on going to."

"It doesn't matter. You're not going now," he says, kissing me again. "Anyway, you've lost your mind if you think I would pass up going on a trip with you."

I nod and step out of his arms. He grabs my arm and pulls me back, saying, "Wouldn't it be more fun if we went together, Sweetie?"

"It would," I say, keeping my arms at my side.

"I promise, Sweetie, we will get you out of this place when I get back in town. I should only be gone for a week." He kisses my forehead before releasing his hold and settling himself onto the couch. "Let's watch something else," he says. "None of this Gilmore stuff." Nodding, I click the home icon on my Netflix screen.

After closing the door behind Maverick, I take a deep breath and relax into my favorite chair. What am I going to do? Gwen is going to be so upset if I don't go, and Maverick will be upset if I do.

I need to bake.

I get up and head to the kitchen, then pull my apron over my head. After gathering the supplies for chocolate chip cookies, a recipe I know by heart, I place everything on the counter and get started. First, I measure out flour, baking soda, and salt in a small bowl.

This trip would be so good for me. I haven't seen everyone in so long. And I just told Gwen I would go.

I mix the butter, granulated sugar, brown sugar, and vanilla extract in a separate bowl.

What am I going to do with Maverick gone? I beat the eggs and add them to the mix too.

Ugh, I really do miss Gwen.

We used to have so much fun together, and now, even though Greg is the only one that hasn't returned to our hometown, Trent, Gwen, and I rarely hang out. We really do need some time together; a friend's trip would be perfect.

I mix the dry ingredients slowly into the wet ingredients, stirring it to create the dough. With Maverick being out of town, he wouldn't have to know if I went or not. He'll be gone for a week. I can make sure I am home before he gets back. I add in the chocolate chips and take a bite. The sugar hits just right on my tongue. What he doesn't know can't hurt him, right?

The oven already preheated, I scoop out balls of dough onto the baking sheet.

You can go on this trip, I tell myself.

I deserve some fun. And to please Maverick, I'll even make sure to never be alone with Greg or Trent. I can do this!

I pop the baking sheet into the oven and then grab the timer, taking it with me to sit back in my favorite chair. Mind made up, I dial my sister's number.

"Hey," Margot answers.

"Hey, could you do me a favor?"

"Sure. What's up?"

"Well, I think I want to go on this trip. It's with Gwen."

"That sounds great! I know it's been so long since you've spent quality time together."

"I know. I've been feeling kind of meh lately, and I think I could use some time away with my friends. If I go, would you stop by to pick up the mail and water my plants?"

"Of course, you know I'm always happy to help. I think a trip is just what you need. Hey! I can even pick you up and take you to the airport."

"You don't even know if I got tickets or when the flight is," I laugh. "You could already have plans."

"Well, if I know you . . . and I think I do, you've already bought the tickets, and you are now second-guessing your decision to go. Am I right?"

Of course, she knew I was second-guessing myself. "Well, I wasn't sure, but after doing some baking, I've decided I want to go."

"Was it the chocolate chip cookies again?"

"Yeah," I say before we both laugh.

"So, where are you going to go?"

"Gwen, Trent, Greg, and I are heading up to the Kenton family cabin for some skiing and shopping."

"That sounds perfect. It's been so long since you've been there," my sister replies.

"It has. A few years actually."

"Wow! It is about time then."

"I know, that's why I'm making you drive me to the airport so I can't change my mind."

"Done."

"And you are getting some cookies as a thank you for taking me to the airport."

"I will happily take those cookies off your hands!" she laughs.

"My flight leaves at 1:00 p.m., so I'll need to leave my place around 10:00 a.m. Is that too early for you?"

"Nope, I will be there bright and early."

"Thanks, M, you really are the best sister a girl could ask for!"

After we hang up, I feel a sense of excitement creep through me. *You are about to go on an awesome ski trip with Gwen!*

Then, my stomach tightens thinking of deceiving Maverick. I shake my head, trying not to think of him. *You can do this!*

I can't do this.

Landing in Vermont, I am immediately hit with multiple texts.

Margot sent me a picture of her hanging out in my apartment: *Hi sis, your plants are doing great and these cookies are delicious.*

> **Maverick:** *Hi Sweetie, I know you are upset about not going. We will have fun together when I get back.*

> **Maverick:** *Holly, why aren't you responding? Message me back, asap.*

Maverick's last message came in about ten minutes ago. I shoot him a quick message back.

> **Me:** *Hi, sorry, was working on my latest article. I didn't realize I'd set my phone to silent.*

Sighing, I head toward the car service pickup location. It's March and the roads are nothing but snow and ice. I'm grateful I listened to Gwen and I won't be driving.

"The name is Holly Palmer," I tell the woman at the rental counter.

She clicks her mouse a few times then says, "Oh no, darling, it looks like you're here a day late."

"Late?"

"Yes, we have you booked for our car service yesterday."

Why hello, Murphy's Law, at least you waited until I landed, I think. I should be grateful for that. I reply as calm as I can, "That must be my mistake. Can I reschedule for a car service to Snowden, just the soonest time?"

"Sure, dear," she says and turns to her computer again. "Looks like that will be in a few days."

"A few days!"

"That's right," she says and plasters on a smile. "You could always take a rental car though."

I look out at the snowy conditions. Maybe it won't be so bad to drive. "Okay, let's do that."

"Well, let me see what I can do for you." She turns to her computer screen.

"It looks like I have one car left."

"Great!"

"But it's going to have to be a slow ride because it's a small one. A Chevrolet Impala."

"Oh. Anything that can go wrong will go wrong."

"Murphy's Law?" says the woman at the help desk.

"Yeah."

"The Chevrolet should get the job done though. Want it?"

"Yeah, I'll take it. Can't let Murphy win, right?"

"Right. I'll get you the keys."

As I pull into the lodge at Snowden, I let out a slow, shaky breath. The fact that I'd made it safely here from the rental service in Rutland is a miracle. Being March, you'd think the roads wouldn't be so bad, right? Wrong. Apparently, the roads had recently iced over and hadn't fully thawed out. I lost count of the number of times I had lost traction, even skidding off the road a bit before I was able to right the car. Vermont weather is great for skiing but horrible for driving. My nerves are shot. I should have waited and taken that car service in a few days, but at least I made it in one piece. I take the keys out of the ignition and step out of the car to grab my suitcases.

The streets look as if a powdery blanket of snow had just settled over everything. It's beautiful.

Snowden, Vermont, is the home of a quaint ski village with some of the best ski slopes in the state. Part of its charm is that cars are not allowed. Everyone has to park at the main village entrance and walk or snowmobile to their cabins. And since I'm the first to arrive, that means I'll have to drag my suitcases through the snow to the cabin. I may have survived the drive, but walking in the snow and ice might kill me.

The layers of snow make it so I can't see where the road meets the sidewalk. Every step I take breaks the pristine landscape around me. Evergreen trees look like they've been dipped in icing. The roofs of the cabins I pass are packed full of snow, not a shingle in sight. I manage good time getting to the Kentons' cabin regardless of the deep steps I have to take and the weight of my bags slowing me down.

It's been years since I've been to the Kenton cabin. The last time I came up was when Gwen and I had our first winter break in college. Before that, I used to come once a year with her family. We'd ski, sled, hike, zip-line, and go to outdoor concerts. Being at this cabin brings back so many memories.

You did it! I tell myself as I walk up to the front door.

Not two seconds later, my right foot sinks farther down than I'd anticipated and I trip, falling face-first into the snow.

Well, I almost did it. Lately, it has seemed like Murphy's Law is the theme for my life. Why does everything happen to me? Could this trip get any worse? *No, don't think that or the universe will accept the challenge, I think.* Murphy always finds a way to get me down. Literally, this time.

"You okay?" comes a very warm, very attractive male voice.

Scrambling to my feet, I glance up quickly, and my eyes grow as big as saucers. Greg Kenton is standing in front of me. My hair is full of snow, and I yelp as some slides inside the back of my shirt. "I didn't think anyone was here yet." I shake my head, trying to get the snow out of my hair.

With a smile going up to his eyes, Greg says, "Hi, Palmer, you need some help with your bags?"

I just stand there blinking at him, and when he calls me by my last name again, I do a double take. The crinkle in Greg's eyes paired with the beanie atop his dark brown hair bring me back to our childhood. Gangly, kind Greg is now tall, dark, and handsome Greg.

I know it's only been a few years, but the man standing in front of me holding one of my bright pink suitcases in his muscular arms, shirt taut against his chest, is a far cry from the man I remember from a few years ago.

I immediately grow red, groaning inwardly. I knew he would be here eventually, but Gwen didn't mention he'd be here already!

"Hi, Kenton," I say, "I didn't think you'd be here until later." Suddenly tears pool in my eyes. I turn my face, not wanting him to see me cry. Here I am covered head to toe in snow after having what is probably one of the most stressful and embarrassing days in recent weeks. Why do I ever leave the apartment? Why do I tempt fate to deal me a fair hand? It's been such a rough day, and I wasn't planning to be around someone tonight. What would Maverick think about me spending the night with Greg sleeping only a few doors away? I wipe a tear from my cheek. Why am I so emotional?

"Let me get your things," Greg says, gathering my other suitcase from the snow.

Wearily, I nod.

As I walk inside, I see the same stone fireplace taking over the middle of the cabin, and a lump forms in my throat. A warmth of familiarity hits me hard. The fireplace is not only melting the snow on the outside but also warming something within me. I take my coat, hat, and boots off by the door and rush to sit next to the fire, letting it warm my soul. I feel at home, safe. It's been years since I've felt this way.

I glance over at Greg, who is still hovering by the door. I can't believe he is already here. It's been years since we've been around each other. It will be good to catch up, but not without Gwen. If Maverick finds out I'm here alone with Greg, he'll be furious. Maybe I should have listened to Maverick and not come.

CHAPTER 2
Greg

I watch Holly as she warms her hands by the fireplace. The speckles of snow in her chestnut brown hair melt away as the fire warms her. The pink of cold on her cheeks turns slowly red as the warmth seeps into her skin. The fireplace behind her gives off a glow, causing her eyes to glisten as the flames spark behind her. It's been years since I've seen her, but I have the same reaction as I did then—I can't take my eyes off her.

"So," I say, moving to the couch across from the fireplace, "Gwen didn't mention you were getting here today. If I would've known, I could've picked you up on the snowmobile."

Sighing, Holly closes her eyes, pressing her fingers to her temple. "She didn't mention you were going to be here either. And she's definitely going to get an earful about that," Holly finishes in a mumble as she continues to massage her temple.

"Oh?"

"It's just Maverick."

"Maverick?"

"My boyfriend."

"Right."

"He wouldn't like me being alone here with you."

I want to reach out and massage her stress away. This is not how I envisioned seeing Holly again would go. Why would her boyfriend care if she was here with me? We're just friends. And it's not like I can go somewhere else.

I sigh and shake my head. "Sorry about that. I took an earlier flight. I noticed there was a storm front moving in, and I thought it would be best if I got here early so I wouldn't get caught with a delay. It's been too long since I've been to Snowden."

"What storm front?" Holly says glancing out the windows.

"Just a snowstorm." I shrug. "They don't expect ice or anything like that."

Holly pulls her knees to her chest, then wraps her arms around them. Tears filling her eyes, she wipes them with the back of her hand before turning her head toward the fireplace.

"You okay, Palmer?"

She only nods, keeping her gaze on the fire.

"It's going to be fine," I say. "We have the fire going, and my parents put in a really good backup generator, so if we ever lose power, it will immediately kick on. It's not like we'd have to use each other for body warmth."

Holly's face blanches.

"Sorry. It was just a joke." I mentally kick myself.

Holly looks at me, and our eyes lock. A crease appears on her forehead. "I should have waited to get here after Gwen," she says. "Or I should have listened to Maverick and never come in the first place. He is going to be so mad when he finds out I'm here alone with you." She pauses, frozen at her confession.

"It's just me," I say calmly. "Why would he be so mad that you're meeting up with a friend?"

Sighing, she glanced toward the fire. "Well, Maverick and I typically go on trips together. He asked me to wait until his work trip was over so he could come out here too, but I really wanted to come, and I missed Gwen and you boys too. But now it's just you and me. Maverick's just not going to like it."

"Everything will be fine. I promise Maverick has nothing to worry about."

"I know. He knows we're just friends."

"I'm sure Gwen will be here first thing in the morning."

"Assuming the weather cooperates, which, knowing Murphy, it won't," she sighs.

"What?" I ask, confusion etching across my face. "Who's Murphy?"

Holly giggles. It's music to my ears. "Murphy, as in Murphy's Law. It's my curse. Basically, if anything can go wrong in my life, it will."

I nod skeptically.

"Just trust me, okay."

How do I respond to that? I'm ecstatic that she's here with me. I don't know about Murphy's Law, but I'm thinking it is fate that allowed us both to be here at the same time alone.

Deciding it best not to share any of that, I say, "You want me to show you your room? I don't know when you were here last, but my mom and dad are remodeling. They're still working on the downstairs bedrooms, so we'll only be able to use the upstairs rooms this week."

Holly stands up from the hearth. "That would be great," she says. "I should probably be getting unpacked. I unfortunately have an article I have to finish." She runs her hands through her hair, her arms lifting slightly, showing her midriff.

I can't help but look. *Easy, buddy, she's clearly had a rough day. Avert your eyes, look anywhere else.* I don't need to be caught ogling her.

A second later, Holly turns toward me, and I quickly glance at her bags.

"I can help you take your bags up," I say, "so Murphy doesn't cause them to open when you carry them up the stairs."

"Thank you," Holly says, and laughs. "I shouldn't be such a weirdo about everything—Murphy, Maverick—but it's been a day. Actually, it's just plain been a year. You know?"

I nod in understanding. I've had a year myself, which is why I'm looking forward to this week at the cabin, especially since Holly is here.

Even now, after all these years, my schoolboy crush is as strong as ever.

Smiling, worry lines on her forehead gone for the first time since she's arrived, Holly nods. "Taking my bags up would be great. I have a prescription for comfy pj's and a warm cup of cocoa."

And there it is, the infamous Holly smile. My heart skips a beat as I smile back at her, trying to settle my racing heart. She seems to light up the whole room when she smiles. I shake my head and reach for her bags. It's been a long time since someone's smile had that effect on me. Taking a deep breath, I lead her up the stairs.

As we go up, I say, "Gwen texted and claimed the first room closest to the stairs. She says it allows her to change out of her cold clothes more quickly after a day on the slopes." I shake my head laughing at my sister's insistence.

Reaching the top of the stairs, I continue, "I thought it best to have Trent take the far room. He snores like a troll, and I had to go through lots of ear plugs in college."

Holly laughs. "I remember those snores."

"Anyway, that leaves the two middle rooms. I took the one next to Trent. I didn't want you to have to deal with being next to that for the week. Which leaves . . ."

"My room, between Gwen's and . . . yours," Holly says, twirling her hair as her eyes go back and forth between the rooms.

As we enter her room, Holly walks around, taking everything in. Each room is a private oasis. My parents filled each one with a large, four-poster bed, with matching dressers and side tables. But the best part is the large picture windows that look out over the forest behind the house, giving a view of the mountains and ski slopes just above the treetops. Knowing this window would be a well-used spot, a loveseat had been placed right in front of the window.

"I didn't expect to spend the night with anyone," I say.

Her cheeks turn a perfect shade of pink.

"I mean I didn't expect to have any company tonight." I rub the back of my neck. What is wrong with me?

Her eyes lock with mine, and her cheeks grow redder.

"So, I didn't put clean towels in the bathroom or anything like that," I explain.

"No worries," she says. "I can grab some."

I stand there taking in Holly and her room. I can't believe she's here with me, that we got this little bit of time to ourselves.

"So." Holly looks at me. "I guess I'll get unpacked and changed."

"Right, of course, you'll want to get settled in." I rub the back of my neck. "You mentioned cocoa. Why don't you get unpacked and into some dry clothes, and I'll make some of my world-famous hot cocoa."

At the mention of cocoa, Holly's eyes light up again, making my heart thump in my chest.

"That would be amazing."

"Great!"

"I may need to finish an article I'm working on and take a quick shower first to get the rest of the chill and the airplane ick off of me, so it might be a bit before I'm down."

At the mention of her taking a shower, my spine tingles. "Okay," I manage to croak as I quickly walk out the door. I walk to my room and close the door.

Why am I so nervous? Shaking my head, I look at what I'm wearing and decide to change into something more relaxing, maybe something that will calm my nerves too. I reach into the dresser and pull out some pajama pants. I quickly dress, then wait until I hear Holly shut the bathroom door.

Was I too worked up to see her right now? Yes. Did I need some caffeine to loosen my nerves? Also yes. Now more than ever I am glad that my "world-famous" hot cocoa is made with real cocoa powder, meaning there'd be no shortage of caffeine. I run my hands through my hair, and once I hear the bathroom door lock, I head to the kitchen.

CHAPTER 3
Holly

After submitting my article, I'm enjoying a hot shower. The water cascading over my head releases the tension I've been feeling all day. Today sucked. There's no other way around it. My nerves are shot from driving in the snow. I cried in front of Greg. Oh, and let's not forget the fact that Greg and I will both be here. Together. Alone.

I turn off the water and watch as the steam rises off my arms. I'm grateful that Gwen will be here in the morning. Gwen. Oh gosh, I haven't texted her to let her know I made it to the cabin. I wrap myself in a fluffy blue towel and grab my phone to text her and notice that Maverick has texted again:

> **Maverick:** *Hi Sweetie, I found out this afternoon that my trip will need to be extended a few days, so I'll see you when I get back in about a week and a half. I know you're upset about not going on your trip, but I appreciate you waiting for me.*

My stomach tightens at the thought of lying to Maverick, but I force out a text.

> **Me:** *No worries. Sounds good.*

> **Maverick:** *How's Chessie Valley? You should send me some pics of what you're up to this weekend.*

> **Me:** *It's great. Love you.*

> **Maverick:** *You too. Looking forward to the pics.*

Next, I text Gwen.

Me: *I made it to the Cabin.*

As if she was waiting for my text, the ellipses immediately blink on my screen.

Gwen: *That's great! I'll be there first thing in the morning, enjoy your night alone. Can't wait for our trip!!*

Me: *Easier said than done, I have company.*

Gwen: *Wait, what?!*

Me: *Greg's here.*

The ellipses show up and disappear about four times before her response finally comes in.

Gwen: *I didn't know. I thought he was coming later...I'm sure he will just leave you alone, so you can focus on your article. If he bugs you, I'll just have to kick his butt.*

I giggle at my friend's attempt to be macho. Being nearly half a foot shorter than her six-foot-two-inch brother, there's no way Gwen would be able to kick his butt, at least not without some effort.

Me: *Honestly, I was just surprised when he was all of a sudden there. Anyway, getting my pjs on and I'm going to drink some cocoa, then off to bed. I'll see you in the morning!*

Gwen: *Ok, talk soon!*

I reply with a thumbs up emoji then dress in my comfy pj's and brush my hair, throwing it up into a claw clip. Looking down at my pj's, I smile thinking of Margot. She was so excited I said yes to this trip that she rushed out and bought me the cutest red and pink flannel pj's for the trip. That's Margot, always the mom. Even though she's the youngest of my siblings, she has always been the caregiver, making sure we are all okay.

> **Me:** *Hi M, just wanted you to know I made it to the cabin. Thanks for the pjs, these are super comfy!*

> **Margot:** *That's great! I just knew they would be. How's it going?*

> **Me:** *It's been a long day, and Greg is here, so I wasn't expecting that. I hope it goes okay and that Maverick isn't too upset that I'm alone with him tonight.*

> **Margot:** *It'll be fine. And Maverick doesn't have to know!*

> **Me:** *You're right.*

> **Margot:** *Have a great time. Love you!*

> **Me:** *Love you too!!*

After throwing the rest of my things back into my dresser, I slip on my cozy leprechaun socks that I'd picked up in Dublin on spring break with Gwen and head downstairs. I'm going to have a friendly visit with Greg and then off to bed.

And I won't have to say anything to Maverick about Greg and me being alone. I hate keeping things from him, but I don't want him to be upset over nothing. Once Gwen and Trent are here, I won't be worrying about this. It's always better when we're all together. And Gwen's determined to make sure we have a fantastic time. Stepping off the last stair, I slip and land on my butt, letting out a pained grunt.

Greg calls out, "You okay?"

"Yes, I'm fine." I stand and mutter, "Freaking Murphy."

I find Greg in the kitchen. I'm immediately drawn to his dinosaurs-eating-gnomes pajama pants. The unique pattern initially caught my eye, but the way the pants sit on his hips drew my eyes to his backside. They accentuate it in a way that's unfair to the rest of us non-model-looking people. Wait, I should not be checking out Greg's butt. This is Greg. He's a friend, and I have a boyfriend.

"You feeling better then, Palmer?" Greg asks. "All warmed up?"

"Definitely. A warm shower and comfy pajamas make all the difference," I reply, then quickly glance away from him toward the pot on the stove. "But that delicious-smelling cocoa will be the cherry on top."

"You gnome it," he says, and I laugh at his horrible pun. "Would you grab some mugs?" he asks. "They're in the cabinet next to the window." He motions at a cabinet a few feet away from him.

I maneuver around him, trying hard not to stare at how well his gray shirt hugs his body. I open the cabinet and grab a pair of matching mugs, blue with white snowflakes. These seem good. I need a reason to not hate the snow tonight.

"Appropriate choice," Greg says, nodding at my selection.

Greg adds cocoa to our mugs and tops it off with some whipped cream and a sprinkle of crushed peppermint.

My absolute favorite way to make cocoa. Does he know that I love how whipped cream melts into the cocoa and makes it even creamier? Plus, nothing's better than chocolate with peppermint.

"How'd you know I love peppermint in my cocoa and whipped cream instead of marshmallows?" I ask.

"I didn't. It's how I like it. That's why I called it *my* world-famous hot chocolate recipe."

"Thank you." I take my mug and find a squishy chair near the fireplace to sit and sip the cocoa. The smell of the peppermint and chocolate makes me act before thinking. I take a sip and immediately burn my tongue.

Of course I burn my mouth because who actually waits long enough for hot cocoa to cool down? I immediately sputter, and hot cocoa runs down the side of my mouth.

"Couldn't wait, could you, Palmer?" Greg says, then laughs.

I shake my head. "Nope, I never can. It smells so yummy and I want to drink it up."

"It's the peppermint. Well, that and the cocoa powder I use. I'm not a big fan of the prepackaged hot chocolate. Doesn't have the same effect."

"Well, I get why you call it world-famous. It's delicious."

"Thanks."

Timidly, I chance another sip of the cocoa. Seriously so good, the mix of chocolate and peppermint is perfect. He must have cooked it with peppermint too.

"I heard from Gwen while you were upstairs," Greg says. "She said I should leave you alone so you can work on that article. But hopefully my hot cocoa will solidify a good report from you that I was the epitome of a good host."

I laugh. "Actually, I finished my article. But yeah, Gwen told me to tell you she'd kick your butt if you bugged me." I feel my cheeks heating up at the mention of his butt. Ugh, what's wrong with me?

"Well, be sure to tell me if I should leave. I'd hate for Gwen to pull a muscle trying to kick my butt," he says seriously, all humor gone from his face.

That does me in. His solemn look plus the image of Gwen trying to kick his butt have me laughing so hard I'm nearly in tears. I set my cocoa down before it spills on my new pj's.

I wipe my eyes and take a few steadying breaths. "It's been way too long since we've gone away together."

"Why is that?" Greg asks. "Gwen mentioned that even you two haven't taken time off together in years. You used to be inseparable."

"It's just, well, Maverick. He just misses me a lot when we do things separately. He would rather we do everything together."

"Oh, not even a trip with people you've known since childhood?"

"Yeah."

"Hmm."

I can't believe I told him that. *Don't talk about Maverick right now, just enjoy the company of your friend who is treating you to delicious cocoa, I think.*

Clearing my throat, I change the topic.

"So what do you want to do this week while we're all together?"

He shrugs. "Not much, some skiing and catching up with everyone. Work has been crazy, so I haven't even been able to stay in contact with my friends from New York like I normally do, much less Trent."

"Same with me and Gwen."

"But I finished a big project at work and had some well-deserved time off, so this friend's trip was perfect timing."

I nod. "It sure is comforting to be back at the cabin. It's been way too long really." I take another sip of cocoa. "Now that I'm back here, it just feels right, you know? There's something about this place. It feels like home."

Greg nods. "It does feel like home," he says looking into my eyes. I nod as my cheeks grow warm. Then I pick my mug back up so I have an excuse to break eye contact. The way he just looked at me. I can't breathe. Has Maverick ever looked at me like that?

We sit in amicable silence while drinking our peppermint cocoa and listening to the sound of the crackling fireplace.

After pulling a blanket out of the basket next to me, I rest my head on the chair cushion. I take silent sips of my cocoa. Every now and then, I sneak a glance in Greg's direction. He seems as relaxed as I am. There's something comforting about being in the moment, watching the flames flicker.

From my chair, I watch as the snow picks up. The howling of the wind intensifies. Thank goodness I didn't have to haul my suitcases in that. Large flakes swirl through the air, pelting the windows. The trees quickly fill with snow, their branches shaking at the weight.

Greg was right. It does look like a bad storm is coming in. My heart begins to race, and my hands shake at the thought of the impending storm causing Gwen to be delayed. With a last sip of the cocoa, I set my empty mug on the table and stand up. I need to curl up in my bed and sleep through the worst of this.

"Heading to bed?" asks Greg.

"Yeah. Thank you for the cocoa. It was pure heaven."

"Of course," Greg says, meeting my eyes. "I'll wait for the fire to wind down and make sure it's out before I head upstairs. Don't want to give Murphy a chance to ruin anything else, do we, Palmer?"

"I'd offer to help, but I haven't the slightest clue what to do with fireplaces. I'm probably better off in my bed."

Greg raises an eyebrow, "Are you?"

My face flushes. "I mean I better get going to bed." I reach for my mug, and Greg stands to grab it too. As my hand lands on top of his, the warmth of his hand spreads through me.

"You've had a long day," he says softly. "I can clean up. You get up to bed and get some rest. If I know Gwen, she'll have an action-packed week planned for us all."

He hasn't let go of the mug, and neither have I. I feel my cheeks heating when I realize I'm practically holding his hand.

"I can get the mugs," I assure him.

He smiles and looks into my eyes. He smells smoky but with a hint of something spicy, maybe cinnamon? I love cinnamon, which makes his scent intoxicating to me.

We stand there awkwardly holding my mug until he says, "I promise I can handle one extra mug."

I nod, pulling my hand away and stepping back. I instantly feel chilled. "Okay, well, good night then." I wave and turn toward the stairs.

"Palmer," Greg calls out to me.

"Yeah," I answer, turning back toward him.

"Uh, just, sleep well," he says as he gathers both mugs in one hand.

"Thanks. You too, Kenton." Turning around, I quickly head up the stairs.

Sliding under my covers, I feel my hand still tingle from where it touched Greg's.

Maybe it won't be so bad being alone with Greg for a while.

CHAPTER 4
Greg

Taking the mugs to the kitchen, my heart is still beating from when Holly's hand landed on mine.

I turn on the faucet and add some dish soap to the sink. There is nothing more I want than to pull her close to me. To finally feel her lips on mine.

I put the mugs and pots into the soapy water. Then I roll my eyes at myself. Stupid, that's what I am. I can't believe I didn't ask her out the thousands of times I could have in the past.

I grab a washcloth and scrub the dishes.

As long as she has a boyfriend, I can't say anything to her about how I feel, right? How am I going to be around her for an entire week? It will be torture having her around, knowing I can't be with her. From the first day she walked into my life, I've been drawn to her.

I was thirteen. Trent, Gwen, and I were playing video games when we heard a knock at the door.

"Oh, that must be my new friend," said Gwen, dropping her controller.

"What new friend?" I asked.

"She just moved down the street. Mom invited her over."

"Cool, maybe we can play teams," Trent said, gesturing to the TV.

"I'm going to run out and get her," said Gwen. "Be right back." We didn't have to wait long before we heard the sound of giggling coming up the stairs.

Holly followed Gwen into the room, staring at the ground. Her shoulder-length chestnut hair shined as the sun reflected off it.

"Hi, I'm Trent, want to play?"

Holly glanced up, showing the most brilliant shade of green eyes. One look and my breath caught in my throat.

"Of course she wants to," said Gwen. "What do we have this for?" Gwen grabs a fourth controller.

"What's your name?" asked Trent.

"Holly," she said softly. Turning to me, she asked, "And you?"

My mind raced and my tongue caught in my throat. Nothing came out. *Say something, anything.* I managed a flimsy "I'm . . ." before my brain blanked. *What is my name? Wow, what is wrong with me? Say your name!*

Gwen rolled her eyes, then said, "That's Greg, my brother." She nudged me with her elbow. "Move over, Greg. Make room for Holly."

Gwen motioned for Holly to take a spot on the couch. Holly glanced over at me before sitting in between me and Gwen.

I couldn't stop staring at her. It wasn't until the game began and everyone had crossed the starting line that I regained my senses.

"What are you doing back there?" Trent asked. "Come on, dude, catch up!" I blinked and shook my head, trying to focus.

I was smitten with Holly from that moment on.

Over the years, I wasn't the only one. Throughout middle school and high school, she had the occasional boyfriend. But even when she didn't, I never got the nerve to tell her how I felt. How would she react? What if I scared her away? Or ruined our friendship? I tried many times to move past my crush on Holly, but it never lasted.

It wasn't until I saw Holly tonight covered in snow that I realized I've never gotten over her. After all this time, I am still head over heels for her.

Now that we're older, would it be weird if we did start something? Could she see me like that? Has she ever? Or would I just be her best friend's older brother, another one of the group?

She seemed so nervous when she found out it would be just the two of us tonight. What does that say about her boyfriend? What would he say or do if he knew Holly and I were here—alone?

After rinsing the dishes and setting them on a towel to dry, I tend to the fire. I gently spread the contents, working the ashes. Sitting back on the couch, I wait for the ashes to cool enough to scoop out into a metal container.

I could learn to be content being Holly's friend for the rest of my life. As long as she's in my life, it doesn't matter what relationship we have, right? I sigh and shake my head. I couldn't even keep my eyes off her tonight. I don't know how much longer I can be around her and just be friends. It's too much.

It's going to be a long week.

The wind whistles outside as the storm continues to get stronger. Large flakes and sleet are falling. I hear the gentle knocking as it hits the roof. The roads are going to be rough for Gwen and Trent tomorrow.

Once the ashes are taken care of, I head to my room. I toss and turn in bed for hours, my body reacting to Holly being so near. I'm emotionally exhausted. I didn't expect that my whole past would come rushing back to me in the form of a snow-covered angel. Without question, once again, I'm completely smitten.

CHAPTER 5
Holly

I wake up to the annoying sound of my phone beeping, notifying me that I've received a text message. I bet that's Gwen letting me know her flight landed in Vermont. What time is it anyway?

I look over at the clock. It's blinking. Looks like the power cut off and back on at some point last night. Ugh, the storm. Looking at my phone, it reads 8:20 a.m. and yep, there's a message from Gwen and a few from Maverick.

> **Maverick:** *Morning Sweetie, call me when you get up.*

> **Maverick:** *Are you still sleeping? Shouldn't you be up already this morning? Call me.*

> **Maverick:** *What are you doing? Why aren't you responding to my texts? I'm getting worried.*

Making a mental note to call Maverick, I scroll through Gwen's text.

> **Gwen:** *I'm so sorry Hol, please don't freak out! My flight change got postponed indefinitely because of a bad storm. The good news is, I'm not in California anymore, but I AM stuck in Atlanta. Please call me as soon as you get this!*

> **Me:** *You're in Atlanta?! No, you are supposed to be almost to the cabin by now!*

My stomach drops to the floor. This means I'll be alone with Greg for even longer than expected.

Those dreaded ellipses appear and disappear right before my phone rings.

"Hi, G." I slump back on my bed.

"Hol, this sucks! It's been three whole hours, and there's still no news about flights to Vermont. I've been talking to the ground staff, but they're all telling me the same thing. Until the storm passes in the Northeast, they have no way to know when the next flights will go out."

"Take a breath, G. It's totally fine," I say.

"I just wanted this to be a fun time for the four of us to get together."

"It will be, when the weather lets up. Don't beat yourself up over this. You can't control the weather."

"Yet." Gwen says it so matter-of-factly that we both laugh in unison. "Hol, please don't regret coming on this trip. I'll be there as soon as I can, and we will still have a fabulous time."

There's nothing I can do about Mother Nature, or Murphy. Guess he earns himself one more point.

"I promise it will be fine," I say. "Last night wasn't so bad with Greg either."

"So you got your article done?"

"I did, actually."

"Great! So when Trent and I show up, you'll be ready for skiing? Do you know if his flight was delayed?"

"I don't. Maybe Greg will know."

"Maybe. I'll have to send Trent a text."

"What are you going to do about being stuck in the airport?" I ask.

"Not sure yet. I may get a hotel nearby."

"Well, it'll be a mini vacation for your vacation. Maybe the hotel will have a heated indoor pool or hot tub?"

"Yeah, that's a good plan. I've been so stressed. I think a good nap and a soak in a hot tub is just what the doctor ordered. I'll reach out later with an update as soon as I have one."

"Good. And I'll have something baked for you when you get here."

"That sounds perfect."

Gwen says bye and we hang up.

Sitting down on the couch that looks out over the forest, I'm in awe. Outside is even more of a winter wonderland than it was last night. Ice crystals stick to the window, still not warm enough to melt. The green of the trees is covered in fresh snowfall. Everything looks so still and serene.

After changing into some fleece-lined exercise pants and an oversized sweater, I throw my hair in a messy bun and walk downstairs. There is a stillness to the room. Gone is the crackling and warmth from the fireplace. I wander over to the fireplace, looking at it with longing. I wish I knew how to get the fire going. I'll just have to wait for Greg to get up.

Stomach grumbling again, I walk around the fireplace and into the kitchen to make breakfast. There's something so homey about the Kentons' large open kitchen. Looking in the fridge, I find some eggs and bacon. After grabbing some bread from the pantry, I take out my phone and turn on an upbeat nineties pop mix to listen to while I cook. Moving my hips to the music, I pull out some pans.

I place a kettle on the stove and boil the water for cocoa. It won't be as good as what Greg made last night, but it'll do. He was so nice to make me cocoa. I'll return the favor by making him some breakfast. I hum to the music as I crack open the eggs.

I love cooking breakfast. Cooking and baking have always been soothing to me. So even though I have to sacrifice sleep to make a hearty breakfast from scratch, it's worth it. And I do it every morning.

As I place the bacon in the pan, I remember the first time I baked for Maverick. I had spent the morning browsing farmer's markets looking for the perfect ingredients.

When I got home, Maverick was waiting for me.

"Where have you been?" he asked.

"I was at the farmer's market. I bought a fresh batch of blueberries. They're going to be delicious." I set the bag full of fresh fruit and produce on the counter and got to work on breakfast.

Half an hour later, I had fresh-from-the-oven blueberry muffins, a mouthwatering, cheesy veggie omelet, and freshly squeezed orange juice on the table.

Maverick grabbed an omelet and took a bite. He washed it down with a sip of the orange juice.

"I hate pulp," he told me.

"Oh, well, it's fresh-squeezed. I didn't strain it, sorry."

"What a waste of time," he said, picking up a muffin and examining it. "You could have just bought the same thing down the street, you know."

"I know, but I wanted to bake. I enjoy it."

"It wouldn't have all this extra sugar if you just bought something like this at that café," he said, setting the muffin back down on the plate.

How, I wondered, *could something so sweet be so bad for you?* After that, I stopped making elaborate breakfasts.

Cooking one this morning makes me realize how much I've missed it.

I'm up to my elbows in bacon and eggs when my phone sounds with an incoming call. I answer, dropping an egg on the floor.

"Hello?"

"Is that any way to great your boyfriend?"

Speak of the devil.

"Oh, hi. Sorry. How are you doing, babe?"

"Why did it take me calling for you to respond to me?"

"What?"

"You got my texts, didn't you?"

I'd been so caught up in my talk with Gwen, I'd completely forgotten to respond.

"Hello? Holly, still there?"

"Sorry, I just dropped an egg. I was so focused on making breakfast I forgot to respond to your texts. Sorry about that."

"You and your breakfasts. Always distracting you."

"I know. How are your meetings going?"

"My meeting was pushed back this morning so I was just waiting around the hotel. I wanted to check in on you while I had some down time. I was worried when you weren't responding to my texts. But now it's taken me so long to get ahold of you that I don't have time to talk. I'm getting ready to head out the door."

"Oh, well that was nice of you. Hopefully your meetings go well."

"I'm sure they will. Next time I text or call, you should respond."

"Yes, I—"

"Gotta go." The call disconnects.

I turn and look at the mess on the floor. One egg wasn't worth making a fuss over. I'd get it cleaned up and begin again.

I shake my head, not wanting to think about that conversation with Maverick, and turn the music up to drown out my thoughts.

CHAPTER 6
Greg

Is that bacon I smell? My nose twitches at the scent while I lie in bed, stretching as I slowly wake up. Holly must have woken up early to prepare for Gwen's arrival. From the sound of the music coming from downstairs, it seems like they're already enjoying their time.

Pulling on a shirt and running my hand through my hair, I head to the bathroom to brush my teeth. Nothing's worse than morning breath, and neither Holly nor Gwen needs to be assaulted with that first thing in the morning.

With both Gwen and Trent coming in today, I want to make sure that I'm not surprised with their arrival like I'd been with Holly's last night. Memories of her covered in snow and the blush on her cheeks make me smile. I'm looking forward to seeing her again.

The smile fades from my face as I look at my phone. I have multiple missed calls from Gwen and Trent. Well, that's not a good sign. Sighing, I head down the stairs as I read that they'll both be delayed flying in.

Bummer. That means I won't be seeing either of them for at least another day.

My stomach growls, letting me know I've been smelling the delicious bacon for far too long without eating any. I'll quickly get the fire going and then reward myself with a piece of bacon. Or two, or seven. That is, if Holly made enough for me too.

Holly. She's here with me.

Maybe Trent and Gwen being delayed isn't such a bad thing. I wouldn't mind spending more time with Holly, just the two of us.

I gather a few logs and some kindling then work for a moment to get the fire going. It'll take a few minutes for the fire to warm up the downstairs, but its warmth already makes a difference from where I'm standing.

"Oh good, you're up. I made breakfast," Holly calls out from the kitchen. "It was the least I could do after you were so nice to me last night."

I add logs to the fire. "As for last night, what was I going to do? Just leave you outside covered in snow? Gwen would have killed me!" She laughs and I smile. Man, does she look so full of life when she laughs. The sound is music to my ears.

I stop what I'm doing as Holly catches my eye from the kitchen. She looks so comfortable and at ease in her yoga pants. Her dark green sweater makes her eyes all the more breathtaking. Her hair's up in one of those messy buns again, showing off her gorgeous neck. She's dancing around the kitchen looking so freaking adorable. I can't help but smile.

"Thanks for getting the fireplace going," she calls out. "You're going to have to show me what to do to start it. I've never used a fireplace that wasn't electric, and I didn't want to burn the place down."

"Of course. I can show you later."

"Let's eat. Would you get some plates down for us?"

Shaking my head to clear it, I lean back against the doorway, arms crossed. "What, and interrupt your awesome dance moves, Palmer? No, thank you, I'll just enjoy the show."

She stops dancing and gives me a stern look.

I smile sheepishly before heading to the cabinets. I grab the plates, setting them on the island and pausing as I watch Holly continue to dance and sing to the song "Best Day of My Life" blaring from her phone.

I grin, making myself a cup of cocoa. It's going to be the best day of my life if she keeps dancing and smiling like that. I pick up some forks and napkins and place them on the table in the breakfast nook. My soul is the lightest it's been in a while.

I notice how amazing the breakfast looks. My mouth waters as she finishes plating. I can't tell if it's from my hunger in wanting to eat breakfast or from how much I want Holly right now.

"This smells delicious," I say. "I didn't realize how hungry I was."

"Thanks. It's not much, but it's my favorite breakfast. Nothing like some cheesy eggs and bacon," she replies, blush creeping over her cheeks. My stomach flips. I love seeing her blush, the heat accentuating her rounded cheeks.

"Don't forget the blueberry muffins," I say, taking a bite to calm my nerves. Why am I so nervous?

"Thanks, I'm glad you like them," she says, glancing at her plate. "They haven't always been a hit."

"Are you kidding? I could eat dozens of these," I say and grab three more.

Am I being a bit much? This is the perfect chance to spend some quality time together, but I don't want to be over-bearing, especially after what she said about her boyfriend.

I can't keep myself from watching her as we eat and she hums along to the music still playing in the background.

"So, did you hear about the storm and the flight delays?" I ask.

"Yeah, I talked to Gwen this morning. She doesn't think she'll be here for at least a day or two. Was Trent able to get through?"

"No, his flight got delayed as well," I say, picking up an egg with my fork.

"I'm disappointed they're not here with us."

"Me too, but I'm not too worried. They should be here soon." Just as I'm about to take a bite, the egg falls into my lap. I look up, hoping Holly didn't see.

"Need a napkin?" she asks.

She definitely saw.

"Yeah," I say, fishing the egg out of my lap. Ugh, could I be more of a dork? Grabbing a napkin from Holly, I change the subject. "It looks like the ski resort should have lots of snow."

"True," she nods, "but I'm looking forward to hanging out at the cabin. I feel so at peace here. Maybe I'll read one of the books I brought with me. Or bake some more."

"You know you can make yourself at home here. My parents and Gwen would want nothing less. You have always been important to our family."

To me.

"And if I have a choice," I continue, "I vote baking. I like baking, especially the dancing that comes with it."

She blanches at my comment.

"Or we hit the slopes today?" I quickly offer.

Why did I suggest it? Why didn't I just leave her to read and relax alone? The more I'm around her the more stupid things I do and say. I'm definitely messing everything up.

"That does sound fun. Are you sure you want to go just with me? It's been a while since I skied. You'd probably be waiting for me at the end of each run."

"Of course I'm sure, Palmer," I say, my voice cracking. I take another sip of orange juice to clear my throat. "I'd enjoy the company, and you don't need to be cooped up when you have the beauty of Snowden at your demand. I won't accept any answer but," and then in the best girly voice I can muster, I say, "I'd love to go skiing with you, Greg." Ugh, if only Trent could hear me now.

Embarrassed, I gather our empty plates. She must think I'm so weird. I head to the sink to clean up. After all, it's only fair that I clean since she cooked. Was I being too pushy, insisting she come skiing? That wouldn't be good. I don't want her to think I'm another arrogant, demanding male.

"It'd be fun if you came," I say. "Or at least I'd try to make it as fun as if everyone else were here," I add.

At that, she laughs. "I seriously doubt that, Kenton, but you've piqued my interest. Now I have to go just to see you try."

Making her laugh tops the list as one of my favorite pastimes. Why hadn't I done this more before? *Because you're an idiot, that's why.*

"So that's a yes?" I ask.

"That's a yes."

Woot! She said yes! I don't care if we're on the bunny slopes all day, as long as she's there.

"Meet you back downstairs in a few minutes?" she asks.

"Sounds like a date. I mean a plan," I stammer.

CHAPTER 7
Holly

OH MY GOSH. Why in the world did I say yes to Greg?! I scream inside. I'm going to make a fool out of myself. Oh gosh, why do I do this? Maverick can never know. He'll go ballistic if he knows I'm out skiing without him, not to mention with another man.

I berate myself the whole way up to my room to change. I haven't skied for like over three years. It's going to take some time before I can get off the easy runs.

Maverick would really hate my skiing with Greg. But it's just Greg, my friend since childhood. What could go wrong? But luck is not on my side, like ever.

I stop at the thought. Nothing too terrible has happened since I got to the cabin, right? *Except you're alone with Greg, and a freak snowstorm is keeping your best friend from being here with you.* At least no one else I knew would be skiing, so that's a plus. No way for Maverick to find out if no one else knows I'm here, right?

I can do this. Maybe the more I tell myself that, the more truthful it'll feel. Yep, it'll be my new motto. It's just a little skiing, and there'll be loads of other people.

By the time I join Greg back downstairs, I'm a nervous wreck.

Greg, on the other hand, looks collected and excited to head out. He looks like a professional skier with his black ski pants fitting him just right and a gray sweater that looks so soft I wonder if it's actually cashmere. I feel the urge to reach out and stroke it. The dark blue ski jacket fits him perfectly and seems to make his eyes sparkle. His hair is partially hidden by a beanie the same deep blue as his jacket. Goggles and gloves are on, and he's ready to hit the slopes.

Compared to him, I look ridiculous. My ski clothes do not fit me as snug as his do. I feel like a giant purple marshmallow. The only good thing about being a marshmallow is that if I fall on the slopes, and let's be honest, everyone knows it's only a matter of time before that happens, at least I'd have the extra padding to break my fall.

Greg looks over as I walk down the stairs. "Ready for some fun?"

"I think so? Skiing is like riding a bike, right? Muscle memory should kick in at some point?" I reply with a half-smile, half-grimace.

"Aww, it won't be that bad. You'll do great!"

Greg hands me one of the extra pairs of skis that line the wall. Greg's parents thought it was well worth the investment to get a whole wall's worth of skis for their family and friends to use while at the cabin. And they were right. Skiing was a favorite pastime of everyone who stayed here—including mine at one point.

"Thank you," I say, taking the skis Greg hands me.

As we walk out the back door, I get my first clear glimpse of the slopes. It was so dark when I got in last night that I didn't see how beautiful this looked. The evergreen trees are dusted with a fresh layer of snow. It looks as if the heavens sprinkled a ton of powdered sugar over the whole mountain.

Yeah, I don't have a sugar addiction. Anyone would think it looks like powdered sugar, right?

Greg leads the way down a semi-private path from the cabin through the forest. "We can go with an easy run if you'd like," he says.

My phone buzzes in my pocket. I slip off a glove and see that it's a text from Maverick.

> **Maverick:** *You haven't posted a BeReal yesterday or today. What's going on, Sweetie? Are you hiding something?*

> **Me:** *Just been busy is all.*

> **Maverick:** *Busy? With what?*

> **Me:** *Just work.*

> **Maverick:** *Well don't let your job take priority over our relationship. You should be keeping me more informed of what you're doing.*

> **Me:** *I know. I'll post a BeReal soon.*

> **Maverick:** *Good, that will help us get back on the right track while I'm gone.*

I sigh, slipping my phone in my pocket and putting my glove back on.

"Everything okay, Palmer?" Greg asks.

"Why are you being so nice to me, Kenton?" I swipe at my eyes, fresh tears forming.

"What? We're friends," he says, shifting on his feet. "Why wouldn't I be nice to you?"

"Um, never mind. I don't know what I'm talking about," I say swiping at my eyes again. "Anyway, you don't need to do an easy run just for me. You probably do the hard runs all the time."

He's going to be so bored if he hangs out on the easy runs with me all day.

Shaking his head he says, "No, of course not! Spending time together is why Gwen planned this trip. Besides, the easier runs will give me a chance to really enjoy the scenery."

"Okay, fine, but we're doing a mid-level run too."

"Sure thing."

I can handle a mid-level run, right? They're only a bit longer and a teensy bit steeper than the easy runs. Ugh, I don't have a chance. With my being so rusty with skiing, the odds of me not falling are slim to none. Murphy wouldn't allow it. I'm sure of it.

The path isn't too long. Before I know it, we've made our way to the chair lift at the bottom of the slopes. It's so peaceful this early in the day. Not many people are even up yet. They probably want to wait for it to warm up a bit more and avoid the biting cold before they hit the slopes. And boy is it biting! I'm actually thankful for the additional padding to my outfit. I have to remember to thank Margot for that later.

Greg motions to the chair lift. Going up together, just the two of us above a snow-dusted mountain, seems too intimate. Like those adorable couples you see in the movies. But, this isn't the movies, and I definitely wouldn't consider myself adorable. Unless it's adorable to be a completely clumsy, purple marshmallow with big hips.

But it would be even weirder to make Greg take a chair lift up after me when there's plenty of room for both of us and we're going to the same run. I feel antsy.

My hands are shaking as I slip my boots into the skis. Why do I have to be such a nutcase about things? This is fine, everything is going to go well. I can make it through a day of skiing, and I'm sure it'll be fun. Clamping both boots into the skis, I move toward the chair lift where Greg stands waiting.

He reaches out to help steady me.

"Here, come stand this way."

"Thanks."

I take his hand. Greg feels strong and sturdy. I'm grateful for the gesture even if it makes my stomach turn somersaults. I think back to last night, our hands touching when we both reached for my mug. My heart flutters at the memory. What is happening to me? Why am I feeling like this?

Okay, Holly, you can do this. Just focus on getting into the chair lift without falling. We're going to have a good day together as friends.

"All right, you two, get in place," says the lift operator. "You're up next."

Stepping onto our indicated spots, the lift pushes up behind us, and with a snap of the bar, we are on our way up the mountain. It doesn't take long for the beauty of the mountain to sink in. The lift takes us over more of the forest that we walked through. Some of the ski runs snake in and out of the tree line. A dusting of snow covers as far as my eyes can see. A little past the ski runs, the roofs of the village shops and restaurants are also covered with the snow from last night, barely a soul walking through the town at this hour. Over the mountaintops, the sun peeks through, making the snow glisten like thousands of crystals.

"It's so beautiful," I say, looking around in awe. This view immediately erases all my fears and anxiety.

"It is beautiful," Greg says. I glance over at Greg to see him smiling at me. He's so close that I can see his breath in the air as he exhales. Time seems to slow as I watch his broad shoulders rise and fall with each breath.

With the slight breeze, I can smell the pine from the trees below. And then I smell Greg's smoky cinnamon scent. Oh my gosh. How can he smell so amazing even with all that ski gear on?

He puts his arm on the back of the lift seat like he belongs up here on this mountain.

Looking at his arm so close to me, my breath hitches. He looks so relaxed, so calm.

But I'm a mess inside. Why do I want to lean into his shoulder? He looks so attractive against the white background of the snow. I lean back just slightly. Even under his ski coat, I can feel his broad shoulder. I image what they look like, his shoulders. His arms. His torso.

"So you ready for a day of fun?" Greg asks, breaking my thoughts.

"What? Oh, yeah, can't wait." It's going to be a fun day. I can feel it. "And I can't wait to see how you manage to make the day more fun than if Gwen and Trent were here."

"Ha, just you wait. You'll say, 'Gwen and Trent who?' in no time. Who needs those two when we can have plenty of fun all by ourselves?"

"Exactly." I smile back at him.

After the lift drops us off at the summit deck, we spend a few hours doing easy runs. Skiing actually is like riding a bike, and after a few wobbles, I feel the familiar rhythm. Just finishing a slope, I adjust my bright pink helmet and my goggles. I roll my eyes at how ridiculous I must look.

Greg points at the medium difficulty trail called Fair to Middling. "You still want to do a mid-level run?"

"Yeah, let's do this. Fair to Middling, here we come!"

I smile with more gusto than I feel. I can do this. It'll be fun. Fair to Middling didn't sound very ominous. Maybe it's an easier mid-run slope?

"After you," Greg motions to the slope.

At first glance, it looks like it wouldn't be too bad, with only a slight incline at the beginning. Taking a deep breath, I slowly begin moving down the trail. I smile as I create a nice zigzag form making my way down the slope.

It's exhilarating. The crisp, fresh air blows past me as I keep up my steady back and forth. This is amazing! Why'd I wait so long to come back to Snowden? If I hadn't come, I would've missed out on not only spending time with my friends but also remembering how good it feels to ski. I can't believe I almost let Maverick convince me not to come.

I realize this isn't the first time I've put off a trip because of him.

When Margot graduated college, I planned to attend the ceremony and cheer her on. But Maverick had a fundraising gala for work the same day. It was some plated dinner for a charity. We lived relatively close to Margot's college, so I assured Maverick I could attend her graduation and make it back in time for the dinner.

"Absolutely not," he said. "Do you know how much I spent on these tickets?"

"I'm guessing quite a bit?"

"A little more than a bit. These tickets go for $10,000 a plate."

"Oh."

"You know I've been working hard for the promotion I deserve. This is my chance to network and bring in a big client."

"Isn't it a charity event?"

"Yeah, so?" he said, waving a hand. "I can do both, network and help raise money for the charity."

"I understand that, but Margot will only graduate college once. Please, Maverick, she's been working so hard, and you know she and I are close. I want to support . . ."

"You've lost your mind if you think I'm going to risk my promotion so you can watch your sister get a piece of paper."

"I'll make it to both. I promise."

"No, we can't risk it. Our future is more important. You need to be here with me."

In the end, I missed my little sister's college graduation.

I still regret not going. Why do I let him hold me back from things I want to do? From things I enjoy? If he could see me skiing now. I laugh at the thought.

The snow powder flies up around me as other skiers pass by, but I don't change my rhythm the entire time. Back and forth, side to side, it's as if I'm creating a perfectly symmetrical zigzag line all the way down the mountain. By the time I reach the bottom of the run, I can't suppress the grin plastered on my face.

Greg pulls up next to me, lifting his goggles. "How was it?"

"Amazing, breathtaking, exhilarating!"

I'm as giddy as a kid on Christmas morning.

"You had great form." Greg smiles at me. "If you hadn't told me that it'd been years since you'd last skied, I'd have thought you'd been out here all winter."

"Let's go again."

Flushed with excitement, I lead the way over to the ski lift for round two.

CHAPTER 8
Greg

The look on Holly's face after she finishes the first mid-level run is indescribable. I'm so proud of her for pushing herself to take the harder run. She can do whatever she puts her mind to. I want to reach over and hug her, to kiss her.

It's been so effortless spending the day with her. And I'm not being too weird myself. Why'd I ever think the day would be hard?

We manage to get in a couple more runs before more people come out to ski, which causes the lift to actually have lines. Thankfully, the lines go quickly. Gliding off the lift at the top, Holly turns toward me, her eyes large as saucers and her breaths short and quick. Her face turns pale, the blood draining from it in a matter of seconds.

"Palmer, are you okay?" I ask.

"Hide me," she says, eyes pleading.

"What is it? What's wrong?"

"He can't see me here."

"Who?" I question. The panic in her eyes makes my heart shutter to a stop. I feel the air leaving my lungs. I immediately feel protective. Who is she talking about? And why is he making her feel so nervous?

"He can't see me with *you*! Why is he here?" Holly whispers.

A look of pure fear crosses her face. I'm uneasy, tense. Tears threaten to fall down her cheeks, and I grow more worried by the second. Holly trembles, shaking her head fervently and gripping my arms tight.

I look around, frantically trying to see who is causing her to react this way.

She glances over at me and then away and back whispering as she tries to steady her voice, "He. Is. Here. Why? Why is *he* here?"

"Holly? Is that you?" A slim, lanky man in a designer ski suit turns toward us.

"Maverick!" Holly says, her words shaky and uneven.

Oh, this can't be good. And what is her boyfriend doing in Snowden?

"Holly!" he yells, coming toward us and leaving behind a dark-haired woman in a red coat. "What are you doing here?"

I take a step closer to Holly, just in case she needs me.

"I . . . I went on that trip. With my friends."

"I told you to wait."

"I know," Holly says. Her words sound as if they are barely escaping her lips.

"So you deliberately lied to my face, told me you were staying in Tennessee, and then went behind my back and flew to Vermont?"

"I'm so sorry, Maverick," Holly whispers.

"And who is this?" Maverick asks, gesturing at me.

"I'm Greg," I say. "Just a friend."

"Just a friend?" Maverick says.

"Yes!" Holly says.

"Then where are the rest of them, your friends?"

"Gwen's and Trent's flights were delayed," Holly says, "and we didn't want to waste the day waiting around for them to get here."

"Delayed flights? Really?" says Maverick. "You think I'm stupid enough to believe a delayed flight hit when my girlfriend is obviously cheating right in front of my face?"

"Whoa, man!" I say holding up my hands. "It's not like that."

"No, we're not!" says Holly. "I would never cheat!"

"Then what would you call lying to me and vacationing with another man?" Maverick yells.

"I . . . I promise. It's nothing," Holly says.

"Their flights really did get delayed," I add in.

"I didn't ask you!" Maverick yells, nearly spitting in my face.

"Calm down, man," I say.

"You have to believe me," says Holly.

"Why would I?" says Maverick. "I trusted you to be at home while I was on my business trip. And you just flat out lied to me."

"Aren't you with someone yourself?" I ask, gesturing to the woman Maverick left behind.

"What are you insinuating?" Maverick asks.

"I'm just saying, you're alone with a woman, and you don't see Holly accusing you of cheating."

"Kenton, don't," Holly says.

"Are you talking about Carmen?" Maverick says. "As Holly knows, I'm on a business trip, and that's my client."

"A business trip?" I ask. "In Snowden? Who on earth goes on business trips states away at a ski lodge?"

"Of course I am on a business trip," Maverick says.

"I'm not buying it," I say.

"Stop!" Holly grabs my arm. "Please, Kenton."

Maverick glances at her hand on my arm. "You didn't think you'd get caught, did you?" he says.

"No!" says Holly, dropping my arm. "I mean, I'm not doing anything wrong."

"I told you we'd go on a trip together after I got home, and you decided I wasn't worth waiting for."

"But that's not—I didn't . . ."

"No, you didn't, and now you've embarrassed me in front of my client," Maverick says, gesturing at Carmen.

"I'm so sorry," says Holly.

"Now can we stop this little charade and let me get back to Carmen, before she changes her mind and doesn't sign with my company?"

"I'm sorry," Holly says again. "I just wanted to get together with my friends. I didn't mean to . . . I'm sorry."

"I thought you cared about me more than this," Maverick says, motioning to me. "You know what? We're done."

"What?" Holly gasps, head snapping up.

"You heard me. We're over."

"No, Maverick," Holly says. "Please. I'm sorry I lied about the trip, but I promise you, I'm not cheating."

"I promise," I say, "nothing's happened. We're just friends."

Maverick ignores me, eyes locked on Holly. "Look, Sweetie, I need someone who is going to be honest with me. How could I be with someone who lies to my face?"

"I'm not!" she pleads. "You have to believe me!" Her eyes look wild, the desperation in her voice making me want to wrap her in a hug, but I hold my ground. I don't want Maverick to have any more reason to think Holly is cheating with me.

"You've lost your mind," Maverick says. "There's no way I could believe you. I don't trust you. We are done. It's over, Holly." He turns his back on us and heads back to Carmen, gently putting his arm on the small of her back and guiding her away.

When they are out of sight, Holly grasps my arm to steady herself.

Did he really just break up with her? Holly's face is a ghostly pale. My heart breaks seeing her like this.

Taking her hands in mine I pull her in close to me. I hold her tight, rubbing her back. But she just feels stiff against my chest.

Damn Maverick! Why did he have to treat Holly like that? She's too good for him. I'll be sure to remind her of that, as soon as she comes back from her shock.

"Come on," I say. "Let's head back to the cabin." She only nods, her eyes dull and full of hurt.

CHAPTER 9
Holly

Oh gosh, what have I done? I replay the conversation over and over. Maverick wants some space? He broke up with me? He thinks I cheated on him. That I was lying to him and that I came here to be with Greg. Why doesn't he believe me? He has to know it's not true. I would never cheat on him.

Why did I have to come on this trip? I've ruined everything.

When I see the cabin, all I think is *safe haven*. There are too many thoughts running through my mind, but here, here is somewhere safe. Home, safety, somewhere I can curl up and process everything that just happened. I slowly peel my boots, gloves, goggles, and helmet off. It's as if I'm being controlled by someone else.

Greg's talking to me, but I can't make out any words. I only hear Maverick saying, "You've lost your mind" and "How could I be with someone who lies to my face?" Those lines play over and over in my head.

I slowly make my way through the cabin and up the stairs, my body moving on autopilot while taking me to my room. I manage to make it inside my door right as the tears finally burst through the dam that'd been holding them in, pouring down my cheeks like a waterfall.

Maverick is here. Maverick is in Snowden. Maverick doesn't want to be with me.

After hours of sifting through my emotions and the conversation that just happened, I feel like I'm going to be sick. My stomach churns. My head spins. I sprint to the bathroom and sit on the cold floor next to the toilet. How could he break up with me? We've been together for years. Years! I have spent so much time with him, and for what? To lie to him, hoping I wouldn't get caught?

I'm an idiot. I turn on the shower to a steaming hot temperature and step in. And now, Maverick doesn't trust me. Of course it looks like I'm cheating with Greg. I would think the same thing if I were in his position. Wouldn't I?

Why hadn't I listened to Maverick and stayed home? Then none of this mess would have happened. But the facts are that he lost faith in me and we broke up.

The steaming water burns against my skin. I welcome the burning feeling. It brings some life back into my numb body. I hadn't felt cold all day until that one talk with Maverick made my blood turn to ice.

The more I think over my past with Maverick and that conversation, the more the numbness is replaced with a heat. An anger. So much anger. Some at myself for being so untrustworthy. But mostly anger at Maverick. Anger that he'd not given me time to explain, that he'd thrown us away so quickly, so easily.

I don't know what would've happened to me if Greg hadn't been there. Greg, he stuck up for me and tried to explain the situation to Maverick. I hate that Greg got dragged into that. He'd just wanted to go out for a few runs down the slopes, not deal with my drama. This was definitely not what either of us had envisioned for our first day catching up.

But I would've crumpled if he hadn't been there. I am going to have to thank him for that. He was a friend to me when I needed one most.

I turn off the shower and dry off. I get dressed in my comfy pajamas. After brushing my hair, I leave it wet to dry by the fireplace.

As I walk out of the bathroom and head to drop off my stuff, I hear Greg downstairs cooking. I hadn't realized until now that I'm starving.

As I near the kitchen, I smell something delicious. To my surprise, Greg is prepping what looks like a very promising taco bar. I do love a good taco. There's nothing like the crunch of the shell as the sauce drips onto the plate. I don't know if it's the tacos or just pure exhaustion, but my mouth is watering by the time I step into the kitchen.

"Hi," I say timidly.

"Hi, back," Greg says, turning the taco meat over. "Are you hungry?"

"Yes, thank you," I say, twirling my hair around my finger. I feel horrible that he's here cooking me food after I ruined his skiing plans. And I don't think I can eat those tacos, at least not without thanking him. "Listen, about the slopes . . ."

"Look, Palmer," he cuts in, "you don't have to talk about it—about him—if you don't want to. I can't imagine what you're feeling right now."

I held up my hand to stop him. "No, I want to thank you. I never could have handled that without you. Thank you for standing up for me. You're a good friend. I just hate that your day was ruined too."

I pick up a knife and start chopping some tomatoes.

"And no worries," I say, slamming the knife through the tomatoes over and over. "I won't break down crying. I'm all out of tears for the time being. I'm just angry, both at him and at myself."

Greg watches me for a moment. Tentatively, he steps closer and reaches out his hand to still mine.

My hand freezes at his touch. Releasing the knife, I look up at him with angry tears in my eyes.

He turns me toward him and takes both my hands in his. Holding them near his chest, he looks me square in the eyes. "Not a single thing you did today ruined anything. You are *not* to blame for anything that happened. He's a class-A jerk."

I try to shake my head. "Maybe Maverick will change his mind. I can't believe I messed things up so horrendously."

"Stop," he says, shaking his head. "Don't even think that it's your fault."

I close my eyes trying not to cry.

"Plus," he continues, "I think there might have been something else going on."

"What do you mean?" I ask, dropping my hands from his.

"Well, it seemed like that woman he was with wasn't just a client."

"What are you talking about?"

"I don't know, Palmer. I mean, who comes to woo clients in Snowden?"

"Are you saying you think Maverick was cheating on me?" I step back from him and grab onto the counter, trying to catch my breath.

"I . . . I don't know," Greg says, gently grabbing my arm. "That whole interaction just seemed off."

"Maverick cheating on me?" I repeat, letting go of the counter.

"Just forget I brought it up," Greg says. "I shouldn't be adding to more of your stress."

I nod and step toward Greg. It's like something is pulling me to him.

"All I know," says Greg, "is that you are too good for the likes of him."

"You think so?"

"I know so."

This time it is happy tears that threaten to spill out.

"Thank you," I say, "for everything."

Greg takes my face gently in his hands. His thumb softly strokes my cheek. He stares intently into my eyes. It's the most intimate I've been with someone in what feels like ages. After the afternoon I'd had, I can't help myself. I lean my head into Greg's chest and close my eyes, letting out a breath I didn't even realize I was holding.

Greg leans in to me, touching his forehead to mine for a brief moment. "You're welcome," he says.

In this moment, I feel cared for, and the feeling stirs a hunger inside me—one I haven't felt in what seems like a lifetime. I want more of this feeling, more of this closeness.

Our eyes lock. Greg is looking at me intently, longingly. Suddenly he takes a deep breath and steps away from me.

With the sudden lack of warmth, I snap back to reality. The rest of my senses kick back in. What am I even doing? Why am I feeling this way toward Greg? Taking a moment to calm my nerves, I turn back to prepping the tacos.

"It was all I could do to stop myself from saying more to him," Greg continues. "I hate that he hurt you like that."

"After lunch," I say, changing the subject, "I think I'll just hang out here at the cabin."

"I'll stay with you. I've had plenty of excitement for one day."

Why would he want to spend more time with me when I am such a mess? But I don't care why. I just don't want to stay by myself, not with my thoughts and emotions running crazy. It would be nice to have some company the rest of the day to keep my mind off what happened on the slopes.

"If you'd rather me not," Greg says, "that's fine. I understand."

"No!" I blurt out. "I mean, I don't mind you staying. I could use anything to take my mind off what happened on the slopes."

Okay, Holly, cool it. Stay calm and collected. Greg probably already thinks you're a nutcase for how you reacted earlier. He's just trying to be a good friend. The least I can do is work at not being so crazy.

"What do you want to do?" I ask, trying to calm my nerves. I set some taco shells on my plate and try not to look at him.

"Well, we could watch a movie," Greg suggests. "It's been ages since I've just stayed in and watched one."

Thinking of staying in with Greg, I feel light and free. It's the first I've felt that way in a long time. "That sounds perfect," I say.

CHAPTER 10
Greg

I internally recoil at myself for offering to stay at the cabin with Holly instead of giving her space. She just got dumped. What am I trying to do? Freak her out? Mission accomplished.

But Holly had looked so defeated, so hurt. I can't stand the thought of her being here alone. Besides, she wants me to stay, right? I couldn't help but reach out and comfort her. But what was I thinking holding her like that?

Touching her silky skin was almost too much to bear. I wanted more. Being so close to her, the delicious scent of her vanilla-coconut shampoo kills me. I wanted to pull her in closer. And was it just me, or did she seem to need that embrace as much as I did?

I have to keep myself in check. Holly's whole world just got turned upside down. I can't be a jerk too by coming on so strong right after she gets dumped.

I want to be the one she comes to when she's upset, happy, scared. I'd give anything to be her person—the one to kiss away her hurt, her tears.

"Ready for the movie?" Holly asks after we finish putting away the leftover tacos.

"Yes, lead the way." I gesture a little too forcefully toward the movie room.

She happily obliges, walking in the direction I indicated.

As we enter the movie room, Holly stops, scanning the area. "There's only one couch," she says. "Where did the others go?"

Why is she asking that? Is she just curious? Last time she was here we had an assortment of love seats, couches, and armchairs. Now, in the areas my parents are renovating, furniture is sparse.

"Oh, umm yeah." I rub the back of my neck, explaining, "Mom and Dad decided they wanted to redo this room too. They got rid of the extra seats, leaving this one while they're deciding how they want to do the walls."

Holly nods.

Or is she worried that she'll have to share a couch with me? Would that make her feel uncomfortable? Would it be too intimate? I'd happily sit on the floor if it would make her feel less weird.

"But don't worry," I say. "I could just sit on the floor so we don't have to share." I'm so in my head about this.

"Oh, no," she says. "I wouldn't make you do that. Sharing isn't a big deal."

"You're right," I say. "It's not like you'll have to sit on my lap or anything." Why. Why did I say that?

The thought of her in my lap causes my heart to beat double-time. My face flushes. I look anywhere but at Holly, trying to avoid her eyes.

Grabbing a blanket, she sits on one end of the couch.

I pick up a blanket as well, shaking it out before sitting down. I sit close to her but not too close. She's had an awful day. I want to give her the space she needs, but I want her to lean on me if she needs to.

"So what kind of movies do you like to watch?" I ask.

"Comedies, rom-coms, sometimes action or adventure depending on my mood."

"What kind of mood are you in?" I ask, looking over at her. Stupid question. What's wrong with me? Of course she's upset.

"I'm in the mood for something funny or happy."

I want you to be happy, I think.

"Rom-com it is," I say.

"Really?" she asks. "I seem to recall you always leaving the room when Gwen and I watched rom-coms growing up."

"Don't tell Gwen, but I actually like them," I say and then hold a finger up to my mouth, warning that it's a secret. "There's something relaxing about knowing that no matter what happens, the main characters will wind up together and live happily ever after."

"Yeah," she says, "that's the best part. The real-world stinks. It's nice to get lost in a place where two people can find their forever person."

I want to be your forever person.

"Agreed," I say.

She turns toward me.

"I can't believe you actually like rom-coms." Tilting her head to the side, she gives me a slow smile. "Are you a secret Hallmark Christmas movie guy too?"

Holly is so cute, it almost hurts. "Yes," I say, grinning. "But if you ever tell anyone, I'll adamantly deny it."

She nods enthusiastically, her eyes sparkling and her face breaking out in a wide grin. "Your secret is safe with me!" She turns toward me with her pinky out. "I pinky promise."

Feeling like we are back in grade school, I laugh and link my pinky with hers.

I flip on the projector and look through the streaming service. Truth be told, it doesn't matter to me what we watch. I just want to sit near Holly and enjoy spending time with her. We could watch paint dry, and I'd be content.

Man, do I have it bad. *Reel it in, lover boy, you can't have her if you scare her away.*

I pick a newer movie about a pop star who falls in love with an average guy. No friends to lovers or anything. That would hit too close to home for me.

As the movie starts, we both relax. She adjusts in her seat, and I stretch out my legs.

I spend most of the time watching Holly instead of the movie. I watch as she crosses and uncrosses her legs, then stretches out and pulls them up. She looks so cute laughing at the funny parts and gasping at the shocking ones. I could watch her forever.

What would she say about us if we were in a Hallmark movie? I drape my arm across the back of the couch. Holly inches a little closer to me until she is almost leaning into the crook of my body.

When the movie is over and the on-screen couple ends up together, tears are flowing freely from Holly's eyes. She tries to discreetly wipe them away.

"Sorry, I get really into movies," she says. "Books too, to be honest. There's something about them. I just get sucked into the world they create."

"Don't apologize," I tell her, just slightly closing my arm around her. Having her this close feels right. We feel right. Does she feel it too? I look longingly into her eyes. "We've been friends for years," I whisper. "You don't have to be sorry for being you."

She stares at me for a few seconds before she answers softly, "I know, and you've been such a good friend. I've taken up so much of your day already. I just don't want to be a nuisance."

"You could never be," I say earnestly, our eyes locking.

"So," she says, nodding her head toward the screen. "What'd you think of the movie?"

"It was the best I've ever seen."

She hits me lightly on the arm, laughing and rolling her eyes.

"Right, Mr. Macho guy, I'm sure it was. I'm sure you watch rom-coms all the time, don't you?" She turns slightly in her seat to face me and pulls her legs under her. Her shoulder is touching my arm, and my body buzzes at the contact.

"Not really," I reply, laughing. "I'm mainly working or working out."

"I bet you keep busy with your girlfriend too," Holly says, looking down.

Why did she ask that? Is she trying to see if I'm single? Or is she just catching up since we haven't seen each other in so long?

"I do keep busy," I say. Then I lean in and whisper into her ear, "But I don't have a girlfriend."

She freezes momentarily, before grinning and saying, "And you keep busy watching your rom-coms?"

"Yes," I say and let out a laugh. "Occasionally I watch rom-coms."

"Do you like living in the city?"

"I always dreamt of living in the city, and I've got a good friend there." I sigh, shifting in my seat but not losing contact with her. "But even though my friend and I are close, I'm kind of sick of the city. It's loud, packed with people, and the wind bites at you. What about you? You like living back home?"

She nods. "After college, Maverick was always traveling for work. I got lonely. I wanted to live in a place I was used to, so I went back to Chessie Valley pretty soon after graduating." She pulls her knees up to her chest, lost in thought.

She looks crushed. Just talking about Maverick must have made her upset.

Without thinking, I reach over and gently rub her back. Holly doesn't move. Maybe that means she's okay with me doing this. "I can understand the loneliness," I say, moving my hands in circles.

After a moment, she relaxes into the backrub.

"I thought the city would be this amazing place, but it's really not," I say.

Keep it friendly, Greg. Friends, that's what we are.

I close my eyes, leaning my head back against the couch as I continue to rub her back. Holly leans farther into me. We stay that way, companionable silence surrounding us as we enjoy each other's presence.

I wake with a jolt. Holly's head rests against my shoulder as she sleeps. I check the time and see that it's late. It's been such a long, exhausting day for her, so I decide not to wake her.

And even though I want badly to hold her all night while she leans against me, I need to keep myself in check. I adjust slightly to allow her to lie down on the couch. Standing, I stretch and look over at her. She looks so calm and at ease. I grab the blanket I'd been using and arrange it to cover her. I softly brush the loose strands of hair away from her face.

"Good night, Holly. Sleep well," I whisper and then head to my bedroom.

CHAPTER 11
Holly

Waking up, I feel relaxed and cozy. There are still stars shining outside. It takes me a moment to remember where I am and why I'm here, but when I do, I smile. It was so easy to talk to Greg after the movie. And that back rub was so soothing.

I untangle myself from the blankets. Standing, I begin to fold them, and then pause when I smell Greg's smoky cinnamon scent coming from his blanket. He must have given it to me before he left.

It's been so many years since we've seen each other. He's definitely grown into a man. His working out has paid off; he has muscles in all the right places.

Wait, why am I thinking about Greg like this? We're just friends, aren't we?

I put the blankets back in the basket and look at the time. It's 4:23 a.m., so I could manage a few more hours of sleep. But first, I'm in need of a warm glass of milk.

Shivering, I head into the kitchen and place a small pot on the stove. The scent of smokiness and cinnamon from Greg's blanket stays with me.

I pour some milk into a pot. My senses are wrapped up in the memory of me leaning against Greg. Pulling a mug out of the cabinet, I place it by the stove while I stir the milk. I want to be back in that moment with Greg. Without thinking, I grab the cinnamon out of the pantry and sprinkle some in the milk. The aroma is calming. The tension in me eases slightly.

I've never used cinnamon in my milk before. But this smells so right and keeps the memory of Greg close to me.

I turn the burner off, pour myself a glass, and take a sip of the warmed milk. It hits just the spot. Still holding the mug to my mouth, I turn.

Immediately, I freeze. My breath hitches.

Greg stands not five feet from me. It's as if I summoned him by thinking of his smoky cinnamon scent.

He stands still as a statue. Shirtless. His six pack is in full view. It leads to a sexy abdominal v-line half hidden by his pajamas.

He looks good. More than good. How is it even possible for someone to look so flipping hot?

Neither of us say anything, both taking quick, shallow breaths. My eyes slowly work their way over the rest of his body. I can't help it. When did the Greg I grew up with turn into this? His arms are buff, his lips are luscious and full, and his eyes pierce mine as I look into them.

Suddenly Greg takes deliberate steps in my direction. Stopping inches from me, he takes the mug from my hand and sets it on the island next to us, never breaking eye contact with me.

His warm breath causes goosebumps to spread out in waves over my body.

He takes my face in one of his hands, then lightly grazes his thumb across my mouth. Electric sparks emanate from the spot he touches. I take in a breath as the current reaches all the way to my toes. I try to remind myself how to breathe. In and out. Slow, deep breaths.

His thumb strokes my lips back and forth, over and over. His breaths come short and quick. I open my mouth slightly. Greg moves his hand to the back of my neck, his mouth mere breaths from mine. Bursts of heat flitter through me.

Feeling like I'm going to combust on the spot, I press my lips to his, closing the space between us. A fire explodes through me. My hands move of their own accord, running up his chiseled stomach, through his gruff chest hair, and ending around his neck.

He lets out a moan, pressing his lips harder against mine. I kiss him back with an urgency I didn't even know existed in me. I don't want this to stop. I've never been kissed like this before. I need him as close to me as possible.

He senses my need, grabbing my waist with his free hand and pulling me tight against him. His warmth completely melts away all the anger, fear, and sadness I'd felt today.

My body tingles from head to toe, electricity shooting through me as our kiss deepens. I feel alive. Wanted. I adjust my mouth slightly to deepen the kiss. To heck with the consequences, I want all of him.

A noise echoes through the silent house. But I don't pay attention to it. My senses are flooded with the scent and taste of Greg, and I want it to stay that way.

Then, I recognize the sound of a door closing.

Breathing heavily, I pull back from Greg. He does the same, looking as confused as I feel.

"Is that the front door?" I ask, smoothing out my hair and straightening my shirt.

"I think so," he says, running his hand over his face and through his hair.

Just then Gwen comes into view.

Greg and I exchange a look. Did she see us?

"Oh, you all are up!" she shouts, dropping her suitcase. "I saw the light on and was confused at who would be up at this awful hour."

I let out a quiet sigh of relief. I'm guessing from her upbeat tone that she didn't notice what had just happened between Greg and me.

Gwen flings herself at me, causing me to have to steady myself in her embrace. I wrap my arms around her and give Greg a relieved look.

He nods back at me.

"Imagine my surprise," Gwen says, "that two of my favorite people are up to greet me."

She turns to hug Greg but stops abruptly, "Why in the world do you not have a shirt on?" she asks. "Gross, I do not want to see that."

"Hi, G, we were just . . ." I'm unsure what to actually say.

Greg glances at my mug on the counter and back at me, "We stayed up watching a movie," Greg says, "and decided to get some milk."

Reaching up to my mouth, I trace the same line he'd made with his thumb.

Greg looks at the ground. My ears turn as red as Gwen's hair as she looks between us.

"Are you all okay?" she asks.

"Yeah," Greg says, and then he turns and immediately runs up the stairs.

"Well, that was weird," Gwen says.

"We didn't think you would be here until tomorrow," I tell Gwen.

"I told you I would get here as soon as I could!" she says, taking off her gloves and scarf.

"Yes, I just didn't think it would be this early in the morning."

"Ugh, don't remind me," she says, sitting at the bar. "Anyway, I was able to catch a red-eye and flew in overnight."

"I'm glad you made it," I say, giving her a small smile. "Listen, it's late. Let's talk more in the morning."

"Of course!" Gwen says. "And let's make sure to make lots of coffee. I'm going to need it."

"Me too," I say, turning and heading to my room.

As I walk up the stairs, I still feel the warmth of Greg's body pressed against me, the firmness of his hands holding me near to him.

I make it to my bedroom, shut the door, and then lie down in bed. I'm so relieved Gwen didn't see Greg and me.

There's no way I'll be able to fall asleep now. Not after that! *What the heck just happened? Kissing Greg? Really, Holly! You just broke up with Maverick.* I can't believe I let that kiss happen. My emotions really are all over the place today.

But before my thoughts spiral even more out of control, I touch my fingers to my lips and smile. Greg and I kissed. Not any kiss either. A kiss that turns your life upside down, the type you never forget. I can't help it. I want to be back in his arms. Though I can't exactly do that right now with his sister down the hall.

As the sky turns from a deep blue to bright oranges and pinks, I finally fall asleep with a grin on my face. I'm no longer embarrassed by my reaction to Greg. I don't know if it's a fluke or if it even means anything at all, but Greg and I kissed. He kissed me like I'd never been kissed before.

CHAPTER 12
Greg

I. Kissed. Holly.

What was I thinking? After telling myself that I'd keep my feelings in check, I go and do that! Did I just ruin our friendship? My stomach lurches, a feeling of unease settling over me.

Oh, man, Gwen's going to kill me. As soon as she finds out what happened, I'm dead. But what an amazing kiss that was. Earth-shattering. It actually might be worth dying over.

I don't want to move too fast, and I don't want to hurt Holly, but I've had a crush on her from the moment we met. A thirteen-year crush. No wonder I'm having a hard time controlling myself. And wasn't she the one to close the space between us? If not, she definitely kissed me back. There's no way I'm imagining that. Did she want me as much as I wanted her?

My mind is racing, not letting me sleep. I have no idea how Holly's feeling right now. I should talk to her in the morning. Feel it out. No, I should give her some space. I'll get out of the cabin for a while. I can go out skiing as soon as the slopes open and work off the jitteriness I'm feeling.

I head to the bathroom to take the coldest shower I can stand before going back to bed and falling asleep.

Before the sun is over the mountains, I am more than ready to get out of the cabin and burn off the adrenaline I'm feeling from the kiss last night. After walking downstairs, I'm surprised to see Trent by the fireplace.

"Hi, man," I say, clasping him on the back. "When did you get in?"

"Just now," Trent says, dropping his bags by the stairs.

"I didn't expect to see you here so soon."

"Flights opened up and I caught the earliest one I could," Trent says. "Didn't expect to see anyone up."

"I'm glad you finally made it," I say, pulling on my beanie. "Gwen got here early this morning, so you're the last to arrive."

"Are you heading out to ski?" Trent asks.

"Yep," I say, thinking of why I'm going in the first place. My face reddens, and I'm thankful that Trent can't notice in the darkness of the early morning hours. "Got to get there before the lines get too long," I tell him.

"Give me a sec to change, and I'll join you," he says, heading up the stairs.

"Sounds great. I'll meet you out back."

I jump off the ski lift. This is exactly what I need. The pinks and oranges of the sunrise are visible above the mountaintops, and the snow-packed trees are glistening. Barely a soul is out and about this early, so Trent and I practically have the mountain to ourselves.

Still reeling from the kiss and worrying about the possibly sabotaged friendship with Holly, I direct us straight to the hardest slope. It's been a few years since I've done one this difficult, but I need the challenge.

Barely waiting for Trent to get going, I take off down the slope of a black diamond run. The steep, forty-eight-percent grade makes this slope more challenging than my typical mid-level slopes. The narrow path doesn't allow for a smooth zigzag form, and that is perfect for me at the moment.

I zip down the run, swerving around the occasional tree or rock in the path. The focus required on this difficult of a run pushes all other thoughts out of my mind. It's only me and the run. My focus is paramount as I stake mini drop-offs and jumps caused by small cliffs and rocks covered in packed snow.

By the time I finish the run, my heart is racing, and my face is stinging from the wind. But the jitteriness from the kitchen kiss is no longer at the forefront of my mind. And I don't have that uneasy feeling looming over me anymore.

On the ride back up the mountain, I notice Trent eyeing me.

"What is it?" I ask in a sigh.

"Something's different with you, dude."

I shrug.

"You're taking the mountain hard," he says. "What's on your mind?" he asks, smacking me lightly on the shoulder.

We step off the ski lift at the summit, and I look away from Trent to watch a bird fly from one tree to another. "I have it bad for Holly," I say.

"Tell me something I don't know," Trent says and laughs.

My head snaps around, fixing my gaze back on him. "You knew?"

"Of course I knew. You're like a lovesick puppy, never knowing how to act around her."

I rub the back of my neck, surprised yet relieved that he already knew my feelings for Holly. "Bet you didn't know that I kissed her last night," I say, grinning slightly.

"What? Dude, are you serious?" Trent says then does a little happy dance. "That's fantastic!"

I burst out in laughter. Seeing Trent's six-foot-three-inch frame wobbling around on skis would get to anyone.

"Well, it was pretty great," I say, "but . . ."

"But what?" Trent asks.

"Gwen almost caught us."

"What!"

"She came in late last night. We broke apart seconds before she burst into the room."

"That doesn't sound so bad."

"And then I ran out of the room, barely saying hi to Gwen and leaving Holly to deal with it alone."

"Oh," says Trent. "That is bad, dude."

"I know. They both probably think I am a lunatic." I sigh, running a gloved hand over my face.

"Aww, don't be so hard on yourself. I'm sure it will all blow over," Trent says. He adjusts his ski goggles and then turns to me. "Wait, isn't she still seeing that guy?" Trent asks.

My hands clench at the thought of Maverick.

"No, they broke up . . . earlier in the day."

"Earlier in the day!" Trent exclaims. "You mean the same day that you kissed her?"

"Yeah," I say, staring at my gloves.

"Dang, dude, isn't that a bit soon?" Trent stares at me in shock. "Wasn't she with him for, like, years?"

"It's not like I planned on it," I say. "We ended up being in the kitchen together in the middle of the night, and the kiss just sort of happened."

"In the middle of the night?"

"Yeah, it's a long story, but basically, I was tossing and turning all night because I was thinking about her and the way her ex talked to her. I went to the kitchen to get something to drink, and there she was." I smile, thinking of everything that happened next. "And then we kissed."

"You do have it bad!" Trent says, punching me in the arm.

My face reddens, but I keep smiling. "I know I do. And I know it wasn't the best timing, but in all honesty, her boyfriend was a jerk."

"Yeah, I've heard," says Trent.

"He accused us of cheating and then broke up with her."

"Were you cheating?"

"No! Of course not!" I say. "We hadn't done anything."

"Until after they were broken up?" Trent asks.

"Right. She tried to explain we were just friends, but he wouldn't listen. The way he treated her and the things he said to her were just awful."

I run my hand through my hair, frustrated at the thought of that interaction. Holly deserves so much better.

"Wow. . . . I had no idea it was that bad," Trent says.

"I don't think any of us knew the full extent," I say. "Gwen had an idea he was a jerk, but how could Holly have stayed with him all this time if he treated her like that?"

"I don't know, dude, but she definitely deserves better," Trent says.

"And to make matters worse, I think Maverick was cheating on her."

"What?"

"Yeah. There was this other woman there."

"Another woman? And he accused Holly of cheating? Did Holly know who she was?"

"Yeah, another woman, and no, Holly had no clue. Maverick claimed she was his client." I scoff.

"And you don't think she was?"

"Nope. If I were a betting man, I'd bet everything that he was cheating on Holly with this woman."

"Did you catch him doing something?"

"Not really. It was more of just a gut feeling."

"Dang, man. Then to have him throw it back that Holly was cheating, that's rough."

"Now I've gone and messed things up with her," I say, putting my face in my gloves. "I just want a chance at a relationship with her. I don't want to force her hand. And I don't want to be a rebound, a quick fling in the moment while her emotions are all over the place."

Trent nods.

"I want her to want it too," I say. "But I know it's not fair of me to ask that of her right now. So yeah, I had pent-up energy and came skiing as soon as I could just so I wouldn't have to face her when she woke up." I shake my head.

"Dude, you've got to stop doing that."

"Doing what?"

"Not telling her how you feel every time it gets complicated."

"I know."

"If you want this to work with Holly, you need to talk to her. And don't wait too long. You've had a crush on her forever."

"Thirteen years."

"Jeez, man!" Trent says. "Talk to her! You don't want to have just a crush for another thirteen years, do you?"

"No, I don't," I say. I definitely do not. "I'll talk to her."

"Good. Now let's hit some more slopes!"

CHAPTER 13
Holly

When I wake up, I want to process how I'm feeling from last night, so I decide to bake. There's so much to take in. I don't have a boyfriend anymore. The kiss. Oh, that kiss. I bite my lip to keep myself from breaking out into a wide grin. Ugh, why is Greg making me feel so hot and bothered? Just thinking about him has me tingling all over.

I get out a mixing bowl and whisk. After setting the bowl on the counter, I see the cinnamon left out from last night. Why does Greg's smoky cinnamon scent get to me so much? I can't stop thinking about him and how good he smells.

I pick up the cinnamon shaker and roll it in my hands. Maybe if I bake some snickerdoodles, I can get my cinnamon fill, and his scent won't be so intoxicating. Maybe I won't desire him at all after this.

Desire? Yes. I mean, that is the right word. I desire Greg. I don't know if it's the breakup with Maverick, the proximity to Greg, or our time just the two of us at the cabin. Together. Alone.

"You're baking!" says Gwen, walking into the kitchen.

I nod.

"Processing something?" she asks.

"How did you know?"

Gwen laughs. "Because I know you," she says. "If you're baking, you're thinking about something."

Turning to preheat the oven, I smile. "You do know me."

"So what is it this time?" she asks.

I take a deep breath. Where do I even begin? What should I tell her and keep to myself? There's just so much going on, and it's so complicated. Just telling her about the breakup with Maverick will be difficult. And I can't imagine that she'll understand me kissing her brother—wanting her brother. What if it ruins our relationship? I can't handle this right now. I just can't tell her everything. My eyes unexpectedly fill with tears.

"Oh, Hol," says Gwen, wrapping me in an embrace.

I hug her for a moment, and then I gather my emotions and tell her about the slopes, lying to Maverick about coming on the trip, and him breaking up with me.

"I can't believe this," says Gwen, pacing angrily around the kitchen. "But to be honest, I really am glad that you aren't with that D-bag anymore."

I sigh, breaking the eggs and adding them to the sugar mixture. "I'm not sure what to feel. I'm sad that he was able to break things off with me so easily. I honestly thought we'd be getting married at some point. How could he think I would cheat on him? And how could he not trust me?"

"I understand it's still new and fresh for you, but seriously, Hol, you are so much better off without him."

"You think so?" I slowly add in the dry ingredients, making sure to mix it all evenly.

"Yes!" says Gwen, throwing her hands in the air. "He wasn't good for you. He kept you from your friends and family. Look around, Hol, you had to lie to him to come on this trip and spend time with us."

"You're right," I say. I had never thought of it that way. Had Maverick kept me from some of the most important people in my life? I pour the last of the dry ingredients and mix everything together, scraping the sides of the bowl.

"I don't see why you feel so attached to him," Gwen says.

How could I not see it? "We did spend less time together after Maverick and I started dating."

"I know. You always had to cater to him. When was the last time he did something, anything, you wanted to do? When was the last time he put you first?" Gwen asks.

"I honestly don't know. . . ." I furrow my brows as I ball the cookie dough. "It's been a while."

"That's putting it lightly. You were only happy if he was happy. It always had to be his way or the highway."

I nod, thinking back on so many instances where that was true. He was always taking, never giving.

"Margot and I have been trying to tell you this for years," says Gwen.

"I know," I say. "Maverick treated me like a princess at the beginning of our relationship. I guess somehow over time that changed."

"He was a jerk to you, Hol. Honestly, this breakup is the best thing that could have happened. You are so much better off without him. It only would've gotten worse from here. You don't deserve that."

"I don't, do I?" I roll the dough balls in the cinnamon-sugar mixture, place them on the cookie sheets, and then pop them in the oven.

Funny how I overlooked all the awful memories when I was with him. How could I have missed the signs?

Soon I am pulling the first batch of cookies out of the oven, and I hear Greg and Trent come in through the mudroom.

Greg.

I haven't seen him since our kiss. My stomach flips. How am I going to react when I see him? What do I say? What do I do?

"It smells delicious in here," says Greg, walking into the kitchen. There he is. I can't help but smile. He's sweet and caring, charming and sexy, handsome and sexy, oh wait. . . . I think I mentioned that already. He's also a good listener and has always seemed to truly care for his family and friends.

I may not be family, but I'm definitely a friend. But what are we after that kiss this morning? More than friends? Or was it just a kiss?

Trent's and Greg's faces are red and their hair is disheveled. They must have gone skiing early this morning.

"Great!" says Trent walking around the island. "They're baking. Holly, you make the best desserts!"

"You're here!" Gwen says.

"When did you get in?" I ask.

"Too early this morning," he says.

I smile at Trent. "And you didn't wake us up? How'd you manage that?"

He shrugs, laughing. "Greg warned me Gwen got in early. Didn't want to wake the bear."

Gwen hits him lightly on the arm. "Rude," she says, trying to hide the smile behind her fake frown.

"I'm so glad we're all here," Trent says, picking Gwen up and spinning her around. Then he turns to me and pulls me into a bear hug. "Heard about the breakup, Holly. I'm so sorry," he says, "but you deserve better than him."

"Of course she does," says Gwen.

I shake off the emotions that zip through me at Trent's kind words. Not wanting to talk about the breakup anymore, I say, "Thankfully the Kentons keep this place well-stocked.

We're free to make practically anything we want." I turn, look over my shoulder, and give Greg a hesitant smile.

Greg nods, then looks at the ground. What does that mean? Does he regret our kiss? My heart races as my stomach drops at the thought. Is that why he left to ski so early this morning? No, maybe he just went skiing because Trent got here. Or did we ruin everything with the kiss in the kitchen this morning? I don't want things to be weird between us now. His friendship means so much to me that I would hate for one lapse in judgment to ruin everything.

I shake my head and continue working on the cookies. "How were the slopes today?" I ask.

Greg looks up at me curiously. "How did you know we went skiing?" he questions.

Smiling, I point to his face. "You have mask marks."

"Oh," he says, rubbing a hand on his face.

"So what did you make?" Trent asks, peering around Gwen to inspect the cookies.

Greg comes around the island to take a closer look too. He stands next to me, our hips almost touching. His close-ness makes my pulse race.

"Snickerdoodles," I say, sliding just slightly toward Greg. "I've just been craving cinnamon recently." I breathe in and out trying to calm my pulse.

"Snickerdoodles are the best," Trent says.

"Yeah, they are," says Greg. Walking around me, he takes a pinch of the cinnamon-sugar mixture and pops it into his mouth.

I bat his hand away, "Stop that. Who knows where your hands have been?"

Greg raises a brow at my comment, and his eyes briefly scan my body, reminding me all too well of where his hands have been. A rosy blush immediately consumes my cheeks.

"Yeah, gross, Greg!" Gwen says. "Didn't Mom teach you better than that?"

Greg walks over to the sink and washes his hands.

"That better?" he asks.

I nod as he dries his hands.

"So, why the sudden need for cinnamon?" Greg asks, grabbing another pinch of the cinnamon-sugar mixture.

"What do you mean?" I ask.

"Well, you had some in your milk last night."

"How did you know that?" I say.

He glances at Gwen and lowers his voice, "Well, I noticed after we . . ." he trails off, and I feel his gaze landing on my mouth.

Touching my lips, I quickly break in. "Right. I left some cinnamon on the counter."

"Yes, I must've seen it there," Greg agrees.

Trent looks between the two of us, and Gwen follows his gaze, quirking an eyebrow.

"Since when do you put cinnamon in your milk?" she asks me.

"Oh, umm . . . I read somewhere it was supposed to help you relax." My cheeks grow even redder.

Quick, talk about anything else. Anything! My brain is blank because for the zillionth time today, all I can think about is the kiss. It happened mere feet from where we're standing now. And Greg looks even more kissable in his ski outfit than he did yesterday half-dressed. How is that even possible?

"So, what've you been up to today?" Greg asks, rubbing the back of his neck.

Thank goodness he changed the subject. I go back to my baking, turning away from Greg. The more I can avoid eye contact with him, the better.

"Nothing much," Gwen says. "We slept in, then chatted over some breakfast."

"Did you all have a good time catching up?" he asks.

"What's with the twenty questions, Greg?" asks Gwen suspiciously.

"Just making conversation."

"I mean, I'd like to be caught up on how you both have been," Trent pipes in. "It's been too long since we've all been together."

"I told Gwen about what happened yesterday," I say, "if that's what you're wondering."

Greg's eyes shoot up to mine. Panic radiates from him.

"About Maverick," I continue quickly, realizing that he must have thought I told her about our kiss.

Greg lets out a slow breath and nods.

"Of course, she never liked him," I say, "so she's happy we are finally over."

"That's right," says Gwen, pulling me into a side hug. "You are too good for him, Hol."

"I have to say I agree," Greg says, giving me a small smile.

"I second that," says Trent.

Rubbing the back of his neck again, Greg moves next to me as I take a fresh sheet of cookies out of the oven. He immediately grabs the first one I place on the counter.

"Hey! Those have to cool down," Gwen says.

"What are you doing?" I ask. "You're going to burn your mouth." I swat at his hand with the spatula, but he's too quick for me.

"We like to live dangerously," says Trent then pops a cookie in his mouth as well.

"Ha, since when?" Gwen laughs.

Within seconds, Trent's and Greg's eyes are tearing up because, of course, I'm right. Those cookies are way too hot.

Trent runs to the sink and spits his out. "You weren't kidding," he says. "My mouth is on fire."

Greg is too proud to admit he can't handle the heat. I watch him as he slowly chews his cookie.

"Mmm . . . so good." He winces and then swallows.

"Your face is bright red," says Gwen. "You're not fooling anyone."

"I think I'll grab another," Greg says, reaching for the tray.

"You will not." I laugh and swat his hand with the spatula again. "I'm not driving your sorry tush to the ER after you scorch your mouth." I put my hands on my hips. "You'll need to wait until they cool down, even if you are acting like that's not the hottest thing you've had in your mouth."

"Come on, Greg," says Trent, "video games are calling."

Greg nods and follows Trent toward the movie room. As Greg walks past me, he leans down and whispers soft enough for only me to hear, "Just so you know, that's not the hottest thing that's been in my mouth."

My ears redden.

Greg winks at me, grabs a handful of cookies, and tosses some to Trent, nearly bumping into Gwen.

"Watch it!" says Gwen, laughing as the boys leave the room.

CHAPTER 14
Greg

I was so worried that our kiss would make things awkward between us, but Holly doesn't seem to be acting any different around me. If anything, she seems happier. I can't get enough of Holly or her baking. So when we get out the board games after dinner, I don't hesitate when Holly offers us more cookies along with glasses of milk.

"These cookies are seriously delicious," I say, grabbing two off the plate.

"I thought we could use a bit more nourishment and music," Holly says, "as we duke it out over Ticket to Ride." She grins and flips through her playlist on her phone.

"And you know I want more," Trent says, taking a few more cookies and sitting across from me at the kitchen table.

I set up the game as Holly picks some mixed station playing "Life is a Highway" by Rascal Flatts.

Gwen hums along to the song as we set up our trains, pick out our routes, and begin the game.

"Well, isn't this the perfect song," Trent says.

"What are you talking about?" asks Gwen.

"You know, life is a highway," says Trent. "All the ups and downs. I mean, look at us now compared to the last time we all got together." He bites into another cookie.

"When was that?" asks Holly.

"The last time we were all together?" says Gwen. "I don't know."

"It was right after you two graduated," I say, laying down three cards as I put my trains on a route.

"That's right," says Trent. "Greg had just moved to New York, and I'd begun working full-time at the marina with my dad."

"Greg and New York," says Gwen, drawing two cards. "Who would've thought?"

"Are you liking it up there?" asks Trent. "Away from home and all of us?"

I take a second to look around. My sister, best friend, and the woman I can't stop thinking about are all feathered next to me around the table. "I mean, New York is great," I say. I look at Holly. She's watching me, waiting for me to go on. "But I've missed home and you all."

"Awww," says Gwen, "how nauseatingly sweet."

"I know," I say. "But it's true. I like my job, but I can do marketing from anywhere. I've thought a few times about moving back home and doing it there."

"Are you serious?" says Trent. "You know Dad and I have been begging you to do marketing for the marina for years."

"Yeah, I know," I say, picking up another cookie. "It's just not a decision to be made on a whim."

"I know you're not happy there," Gwen teases, "always answering my calls on the first ring."

"Moving home would be a big change," Holly says, picking up two cards. "It can be a bit overwhelming having so many memories surrounding you wherever you go."

"Some memories I wouldn't mind," I say. "Plus I can make new memories. I've come to realize I'm not the big-city type. I feel more comfortable with family and friends. You know?" I pick up cards.

"Don't you have friends in New York?" asks Gwen.

"Yeah. It's not like being back home though."

"I completely understand," says Holly. "When I was away from home, I felt so lonely. Even though I was with Maverick, it didn't feel the same as having you all around."

"And that's why," Gwen says, "we were so happy when you did move back to Chessie Valley."

"I am too," Holly says. "Honestly, it surprised me that Maverick didn't get all that upset when I told him I wanted to move back home." She picks up a card.

"That really was odd," Gwen agrees, playing multiple cards to lay a six-train route. "It makes you wonder why he let you have that distance when he normally wants you glued to his hip."

"Anyway, enough about my past," Holly says. "I think it would be great if you moved back home, Kenton. As much as Gwen teases, I know she'd love to have you nearby." She looks up at me. "And . . . I wouldn't mind it either."

My eyes light up at her admission. My brain short circuits for a moment, and I lay down the wrong cards for my route before getting called out on my slipup.

"As you said," Holly continues, "it's nice to have friends close by."

Friends? Does she still see us as friends? "Yeah," I say, not wanting to dwell too much on that thought, "it'd be nice to see and talk to my best friends and little sister in person rather than on the phone. A phone call just doesn't pack the same punch. You know?"

The discussion is broken up by a buzzing sound. Holly sets her cards down and pulls her phone from her back pocket. Her face immediately falls. I have one guess as to who it could be.

Maverick.

"Please don't tell me that is who I think it is," says Gwen.

"Fine, I won't," Holly says as she texts.

What was there for him to say to her? Why had she responded? And what did she say?

I want to hold Holly in my arms and tell her that she deserves so much better, that I would never treat her the way Maverick does.

"So," pushes Trent, motioning with his cards. "What'd he say?"

"It's not bad," she says. "He was just apologizing. That was all." She twirls a piece of hair around her finger.

"That better be all it was," Gwen says.

Trent looks at me. I close my eyes, taking a deep, calming breath.

"Are you handling all this okay?" Gwen asks Holly.

"I'm taking each day one moment at a time," she says. "I'll see if Murphy has anything in store for me today. He's been racking up a bunch of wins lately."

"Oh gosh, not Murphy," Gwen says, picking up a locomotive wild card.

Trent cocks his head. "I think I missed something. Who is Murphy?"

"Long story," Holly and I say at the same time.

I turn to look at Holly directly. "Why do you think Murphy's Law has it out for you?" I ask, setting down my cards. "Do you think you made some cosmic misstep and now the world is out to get you?"

"Oh, I don't know," she says. "It's just that since I went off to college, anything and everything has gone wrong in my life."

"That sounds a bit dramatic," says Gwen.

Holly laughs. "It does, but it's true. I'm constantly running into bad luck everywhere I go."

"But this trip hasn't been all bad, right?" asks Trent.

We all glare at him. Did he really just say that?

"Sorry," Trent says, raising his hands in defense. "I mean, besides the obvious bad breakup."

"That's been the worst of it," Holly says. "But there have been other things too, like having issues with the car service company, almost skidding off the road in the snowstorm, falling on my face in front of Kenton, and tripping down the stairs."

"Whoa," says Trent, leaning back in his seat.

"And those are just the little things," Holly says. "Then the power went out here, your flights got delayed, and then . . ." She pauses a moment, twirling her hair again. "And then Maverick on the slopes." She lets out a sigh and grabs another cookie, biting into it.

"Interesting perspective," I say, laying down a train. "However, playing devil's advocate here, what if you've been looking at this all wrong?"

"Here we go," says Gwen, rolling her eyes.

"Maybe," I continue, "it wasn't the universe conspiring against you but rather that you weren't going down the path you were meant to."

"What do you mean?" she asks.

"Maybe the universe keeps throwing speed bumps in your way to try and get you back on your true path."

"This is deep," says Trent right before he practically swallows a cookie whole.

"For example, take your journalism job."

She crinkles her brows at my statement. "What about my job?"

"Do you like what you do? Or is it just a means to an end?" Greg asks.

"I'm not passionate about it."

"I'm guessing you didn't bake much through college or in recent years either?"

"No . . ." she says.

"Get to the point, Greg," Gwen says.

I pick up a snickerdoodle and turn to face Holly. "I've had snickerdoodles my whole life but none have ever tasted as good as these do. Palmer, you have a natural gift. You used to bake all the time growing up. No matter what weird mixture you came up with, it ended up being delicious. Everyone was happy to taste-test your creations. Not to be nice, but because each and every one was always amazing. Every single time."

"I agree whole-heartedly," says Trent, placing another set of trains.

"You think so?" Holly asks.

"You do have a gift," Gwen says.

"We always thought you'd open your own bakery instead of going off to college," I say. "My theory is that you went to school for the wrong thing. Met and dated the wrong guy. And the universe took opportunities to let you know you were going in the wrong direction." My stomach churns a bit. Have I gone too far? What if instead of being with Maverick, she was supposed to be with me? And what if thinking about moving back to Chessie Valley is a sign that now is the time for us to be together?

"I like what you're saying, Greg," Gwen says and then turns to face Holly. "If what he says is true, then that means you were never supposed to feel the hurt and pain you feel from Maverick, because you were never supposed to be with him."

Holly glances down at the floor, cards still in hand.

"Sorry if I went too far," I say, running a hand through my hair.

She meets my eyes. "Don't be," she says, her voice rich with emotion. "You're spot on. One plate of cookies and you've cracked the code. How did you see it, when no one else could?"

"I've known you for years, Palmer," I say. "I see you."

Her eyes widen at my comment, and a smile breaks across her face. "You see me, Kenton?"

Looking into her eyes, I reply, "Of course. I've always seen you."

There's something behind those brilliant green eyes. Something that wasn't quite there before. I hope she's recognizing her talents. I hope she'll use them to be happy. She deserves happiness.

Holly clears her throat, turning back to the game board as she adjusts her cards. "How did we get talking about me, anyway?" she asks. "Weren't we talking about you and New York, Kenton?"

I laugh. "We were," I say.

"So what can we do to convince you to come home?" Holly asks.

My eyes shoot up to hers. Convincing? She wouldn't have to do any convincing. I would do anything to be with her. Honestly, I hadn't moved home before because, well, she was in a relationship, and it would've been too painful to see. Holly stares at me, waiting for a response. Her green eyes look so innocent, so sincere. Does she really want me to move back home? Does that mean she wants to be with me?

I glance around the room at the three of them. There really is nothing keeping me from moving back home anymore.

"Well," I say, "I guess that depends on Trent."

"What depends on me?" Trent asks, abruptly looking up from his cards.

"If I'm going to move back, I'm going to need a job, right?" Greg grins.

"Yes!" says Trent, throwing a fist in the air. "You're hired! No take-backsies."

I laugh at his response. "I guess that settles it then. I'm moving back to Chessie Valley."

"Yay!" Gwen says. She jumps out of her chair, running around the table and squeezing me in a big hug. "It's going to be so much fun, the four of us living in the same town again. Isn't that awesome!"

I look over at Holly, whose eyes haven't left me since she asked her question. A smile slowly breaks across her face and ends in a large grin. "Definitely, just like old times."

She's lovely. And damn do I love to see her smile. Her eyes light up, and her lips are parted just slightly. I stare at them, wanting to feel them against mine again.

"What's with the goofy look on your face?" Gwen asks me. "Are you about to win?"

"Huh? Oh, umm no," I say, looking down at my cards.

"But I am!" Holly says, moving her tracker.

Trent groans. "Man, I'm not even close."

Gwen and Trent both pick up extra routes to see if they can get extra points, but no luck. I use a card to advance one space, but Holly still has the longest train.

"I won!" Holly says, jumping up and down.

I laugh as she celebrates her win, swaying her curvy hips to the song in the background. Gwen laughs for a moment before joining in the dancing fun.

"I didn't know you'd get so excited about winning." I say to Holly, smiling at how happy she is.

"I've just needed a win lately," she says.

After dinner and more games, Gwen and Trent are yawning and complaining about their red-eye and early morning flights. We wave them off as they head up the stairs for an early night.

Holly and I sit in front of the fireplace listening to the crackling of the logs. The heat of the fireplace warms us from head to toe.

"Let's do something," says Holly, looking at me with a playful smile.

"I thought we were doing something," I say, motioning to the fireplace, "enjoying the fire."

"No, something really fun," she says. "Oh! Let's make snow angels." She jumps up and grabs my hand, pulling me from my armchair. "I've been cooped up in this cabin all day."

There is literally no way I could ever say no to her.

"Uh, sure, why not?" I say.

We race toward the mudroom door and throw on scarves, hats, gloves, and coats.

"Come on, Kenton!" She giggles as she pulls on my hands.

"All right, I'm coming," I say, wrapping my fingers around hers.

Opening the mudroom door, we're hit with a blast of cold air. It's been snowing off and on since we got here, and everything is covered in a soft, white blanket of snow.

"Oh my gosh! It's freezing!" Holly rubs her arms.

"Change your mind?"

"Not a chance," she says. She spreads her arms out and falls softly back into the snow.

I follow her lead, landing next to her. The snow's freezing, but somehow, I don't care.

As we wave our outstretched hands and feet to make snow angels, our fingertips brush against each other. Each brief touch causes an electric current to pass through me.

Laughing, Holly gets up and holds her hand out, offering to help me up.

I take her hand and maneuver to stand. Just as I do, my foot slips. I fall backward, pulling Holly down with me. Just before she hits the ground, I scoop her in my arms.

She lands directly on top of me.

Shocked from the sudden movement, her emerald eyes widen. I gaze into them, and my heart beats faster. The feel of her body pressed up against mine overwhelms my senses.

We slowly inhale and exhale in unison. In the cold night air, our steamy breaths collide in the short distance between us. My hands roam over her legs, landing on her hips. I breathe in her sweet vanilla-coconut perfume. Memories of our kiss flash through my mind. Time stands still as we lie together, taking each other in.

"Palmer," I say, tucking a strand of hair behind her ear. "I want to talk about last night."

"Yeah," she says, not breaking eye contact.

"That kiss . . ." I trail off.

"What about it?" she asks, running a finger along my stubbled chin.

"Well, I—"

Suddenly I see a movement out of the corner of my eye. I look up, and Holly follows my gaze.

Gwen is standing at her window. She stares at us for a brief moment longer and then closes her curtain.

Holly rolls out of my arms, and we both jump up.

"We better go in," I say.

CHAPTER 15
Holly

Inside, I head straight to my room and quickly strip off my wet clothes and put on my pajamas.

What did Gwen see? Did she notice how long I was lying in Greg's arms? Did she see the way I was looking at him? For a moment, I thought he was going to kiss me again. And I wanted him to. What does that say about me?

Oh, gosh. I hope she was watching long enough to know that it was all an accident. Greg just saved me from falling and getting hurt, and I somehow ended up on top of him.

What is Gwen thinking right now? Is she upset at Greg? Me? Is she going to hate that I might have feelings for her brother? That I was lying on top of him for much longer than a friend should have? What is she going to do? Will she explode on me? Ignore me?

My pulse races, but not in a good way. I feel nauseous and overwhelmed. Is that moment in the snow going to ruin my friendship with Gwen?

My phone buzzes, and I'm reminded of the slew of texts I've gotten from Maverick throughout the day. I unlock my phone and read through the most recent ones.

> **Maverick:** *Hi Sweetie, I mean what I said earlier. I shouldn't have acted like I did on the slopes. I know you wouldn't cheat on me. I was just shocked that you'd lie to me.*

Maverick: *I just needed some time to clear my head. And now I know it was all a misunderstanding.*

Maverick: *Don't be mad at me Sweetie. I really care about you. I don't want to end things with you.*

Maverick: *I want us to work. How about you come over and we talk in person?*

I mull the messages over for a moment. It really was a misunderstanding. Maybe it would be good for both of us to talk about it now that we've had a chance to process everything that happened. And I do want to assure him that I would never cheat on him.

Me: *Ok, I think it would be good for us to talk.*

Maverick: *Thanks, Sweetie. I'm staying at the Hearthstone Lodge, cabin 521. Take your time getting here. No rush.*

I throw on my warmest leggings and sweater then put on my ski shoes, preparing to walk through the snowy village to get to the lodge.

I pause, thinking about how I almost allowed myself to kiss Greg again. Why am I so drawn to him? Do I want to see if there could be something with him? Should I leave Maverick and lose all the years we've had together over a misunderstanding? We cared about each other so much at the beginning. Maybe I wasn't trying hard enough now. Maybe we could get back to where we were. I need to figure things out. First, I'll head to Maverick's and talk things out with him. I at least owe our relationship that. After that, I can process my feelings for Greg.

Not wanting to run into Gwen or Greg, I tiptoe down the stairs and slip out the mudroom door. The lights on the street are just bright enough for me to see.

It's still freezing out and snow is falling lightly. I shiver. The faster I get to Maverick, the warmer I'll be.

I've crunched through a few streets of frozen snow when suddenly I lose my footing. Arms flailing, I try to regain my balance, but I land hard on my back.

Murphy strikes again.

Great job, Holly. I grimace and then slowly stand. I brush myself off as well as I can, but there's no way I'm getting all the snow out of my hair. At least this time, I didn't fall face first. Stepping lightly now, I continue the rest of the way to Hearthstone Lodge.

The lodge has got to be one of the most expensive luxury cabin rentals in Snowden. Even though Christmas has past, Hearthstone Lodge still has strings of lights and garland over the lodge, giving it a magical feel. The lodge looks stunning. It's a mix between a stone mansion and a large rustic cabin. The mixture creates a fairytale effect. Many chimneys dot the snow-covered roofs, the melting snow dripping away as puffs of smoke show which cabin residences are warming their homes.

Nearly to Maverick's cabin, I turn a corner and run directly into a dark-haired woman. The impact almost causes me to slip again, but I manage not to fall. The woman, on the other hand, does.

"I'm so sorry," I say, helping her up. I feel horrible knowing that she'll probably be as soaked as I am.

"No worries," she says. "No harm done." She stands, brushing the snow off her red coat, and continues on her way.

At Maverick's cabin door, I take off my gloves and knock lightly. Why did that woman look so familiar? Where would I know her from? A few moments go by, and I don't hear anything from the other side of the door.

What if Maverick's changed his mind? What if I've walked here for nothing? I'm soaked; my wet hair drips down my back. I wait a few more seconds before knocking again. Then, I hear the locks turn.

"Sweetie," Maverick says opening the door and wrapping me in his arms. "You got here a lot faster than I thought you would." He motions for me to sit on the couch.

"Thank you," I say, stepping past him and sitting down.

Maverick sits next to me. "I'm so glad you're here," he says, taking my hand.

I nod. "Me too."

He runs his hand up my body and to the back of my head, and then he pulls me in so my lips are pressed against his.

I wince and pull away. "I think we should talk first," I say.

"Of course," he says. "We can save this for later."

I grimace.

"I didn't think you'd want anything to do with me," I say, "after, well, after the other day." I twirl a strand of my soaking hair.

"You don't have to be nervous with me. You know me, Holly." Maverick takes my hand. "I always take care of you."

Did he take care of me on the slopes? No, he made me feel like crap. It was Greg who cared for me. It was Greg who stood up for me.

"I never want to be without you," Maverick says. "I'm so glad we decided to work things out."

"Talk things through," I correct him.

"Right," he says, squeezing my hand.

"Maverick, I promise you that I wasn't cheating. Gwen's and Trent's flights really were—"

"Shh," Maverick says, putting a finger to my lips. "No need to explain. I believe you."

I give him a meek smile.

"We fit. We work well together," he continues. "Let's not waste the last three years. Let's keep us going. Think of all the things we'd miss out on doing together. Going to charity events for my work. Fancy networking parties in downtown Nashville."

I nod and genuinely try to take in what he is saying, but all I see when I look at him is the slopes. The way he treated me and the cruel things he said. The words "you've embarrassed me" and "you've lost your mind" sound over and over in my head.

Then I picture Greg. Greg when he stood up for me on the slopes. Greg kissing me in the kitchen. Greg encouraging me to follow my dream of baking. Greg making snow angels with me. Greg almost kissing me again.

"I may need some time to think about things," I say, "if that's okay."

Maverick lets go of my hand. His jaw clenches for a beat, then he smiles and nods. "Of course, Sweetie. Why don't you call me tomorrow?"

I nod and stand to leave. It's even colder now. My sweater is soaked from my hair. I shiver just thinking about walking back to the Kentons' cabin.

"Can I use the restroom?" I ask. "I slipped on the way here, and now I'm soaked. I'd love to dry up a bit before I head back out in the snow."

"Of course you slipped," Maverick says. "That's such a Holly thing to do. The bathroom is just down the hall on the right."

I give Maverick a small smile before heading into the bathroom.

The bathroom is huge. A large claw-foot tub sits against one wall with a walk-in shower big enough for two people on the other side. I grab a clean towel off the marble counter and begin to dry my hair. I take in the double sinks and mirrors. The brand-name slippers and robes, the soaps and shampoos.

I set the wet towel on the counter and wash my hands. Reaching for a new towel to dry them, I notice something red sticking out of a robe pocket. What kind of fancy accessory could this be? Curious, I pull it out.

It's a red, lacy bra.

My mouth goes dry, and my stomach twists. What is this doing in Maverick's cabin? Calm down, Holly. I'm sure there's an explanation for this. Maybe one of his coworkers had to stay in this cabin too? I'm sure his company paid for it. They wouldn't want to waste such an expensive cabin on just one person, would they?

Just then Maverick knocks on the bathroom door.

"You fall in?" he asks, trying the handle. Luckily, I had locked it.

"Just drying my hands," I answer, shoving the bra back in the robe pocket. I leave the bathroom to find Maverick standing right outside the door. He glances over my shoulder as he takes my arm, leading me back to the living area.

Maverick pulls me in for another embrace, but I'm stiff. My head is spinning, and I feel sick. "Think about what we talked about, okay?" Maverick says. "I miss you, Sweetie, and hope we can get past your little outburst and lies." He plants another kiss on my forehead.

I don't feel anything.

I smile meekly and slip out the door.

CHAPTER 16
Greg

It's been an hour or so since Gwen caught Holly and me in the snow. I'm pacing in front of the fireplace. I haven't heard a thing from Holly. I hope she's doing okay. I hope Gwen isn't too upset about seeing us. I hope Holly doesn't regret whatever is happening between us. I hope she doesn't get scared off. What if she just packs up and leaves tonight because it's too much? I take a deep breath and watch the fire. I need to calm down, get a hold of myself.

Then I hear footsteps on the stairs. My heart races. Is Holly coming down to talk through everything with me? I smile with relief and turn my head.

A furious redhead stares me down.

"Hi, Gwennie," I say. Great. She's the last person I want to see right now.

"Don't," she says. "Don't just 'Hi, Gwennie' me. I saw you. I know you saw me too. What do you think you were doing?" She places her hands on her hips, looking very much like our mother when she scolds us.

I don't want to answer her. I'm not ready for Gwen to know about my feelings for her best friend. Not yet. Not before I can figure out what Holly is feeling. "Making snow angels," I offer half-heartedly, knowing full well Gwen won't buy it.

"Really?" she says, "That's what you're going with?"

I don't respond.

"Do you know what it looked like to me, Greg? It looked like you were holding my best friend in your lap."

"We'd been making snow angels before that," I say, then run a hand through my hair. "We were about to come in, and then I slipped, and Holly came down with me."

A flicker of anger crosses Gwen's face. She shakes her head and stares me down. Even though she's my little sister, she can be terrifying.

"Look, nothing happened, okay. We just went outside to make snow angels, slipped and fell, then came back inside. She went to bed, and I've been waiting for the fire to burn out."

"Greg," Gwen says, calming slightly. "Holly is my friend."

"Yeah, and she's my friend too, Gwennie."

"I know we are all friends," she snaps. "That is not what I meant, and you know it."

She takes a lap around the living room. I push around the last of the ashes, waiting for her to continue. She paces for a few more minutes before sitting down in the chair next to me.

"I know what I saw, even if you don't want to admit there is anything happening. I know you, Greg. That was more than just a slip. She is my friend—our friend. I don't want anything to mess that up. I can't lose her again. Not after we just got her back."

We sit there in silence for a few minutes. Finally, Gwen asks, "Well, are you going to say anything?"

I let out a breath. *Okay, Greg, she's your sister and she loves you. She only wants what's best for you and Holly both.* "I want you to know that I haven't ever lied to you," I say. "I just may have kept some things from you."

"Mmhmm," she says unamused, "go on." I avoid looking at her because I don't want to lose my nerve.

I run my hands through my hair before continuing, "I have feelings for Holly."

"I knew it!" Gwen says. "I can't believe this! I can't believe you'd risk our friendships and—"

"Please, Gwennie," I say, meeting her eyes, "let me explain."

She clenches her jaw but nods.

"I have feelings for Holly, but these aren't new feelings. I've cared for her since the first day we met. At first, I didn't think it was serious. But now, after spending these last few days with her, I've realized my feelings are so much more real and strong than I thought. I really like her, Gwennie. Like, really like her."

I rub the back of my neck. Am I messing everything up by sharing my feelings with Gwen? Could she ever see it from my perspective? Could she ever be okay with me pursuing her best friend?

Gwen lets out a breath. "Does Holly know?"

"I'm not sure. I mean, she's got to have some idea. I haven't exactly been subtle."

"That's for sure," Gwen says.

"But please don't say anything to Holly," I say. "I want to talk to her, let her know how I really feel."

"She just broke up with the D-bag. You can't seriously be thinking of asking her out," Gwen says.

I shake my head. "Not exactly. I want to have time with her to feel things out a little more. I want her to realize that she deserves better than Maverick."

"And better would be you?" Gwen asks.

"I'm hoping," I say. "But I need your help."

"Me, why? I'm not talking you up to her if that's what you're asking." She puts a hand on her hip.

I laugh and say, "No, nothing like that. I just want you to be okay with this and maybe give me some time alone with her."

"Well, I'm not letting you take her all to yourself while we're here. She's my best friend, and I came on this trip to spend it with her, not push her into a relationship with my brother."

"I know. I just mean maybe when I ask for it, you'll be okay with me going off with her, just the two of us, to talk about what we could be."

My heart beats frantically as I wait for Gwen to think through everything I've told her. So much relies on Gwen's approval.

"I promise I won't hurt her, Gwennie. I could never live with myself if I did."

"I know you couldn't," Gwen says. "You just never know how these things are going to turn out."

I nod.

Gwen looks at me hard before saying, "It makes me so happy that Holly and Maverick are over. But I hate that I couldn't stop him from hurting her and from ostracizing her from her friends and family—from her dreams. I don't want to see her hurt again."

"I wouldn't hurt her. I would treat her right, Gwen."

"Just the two of you together makes things messy. What if things are great for a while, but then they aren't, and you have a terrible breakup, and I'm caught in the middle having to choose between my brother and my best friend?" Gwen shakes her head.

"I get it," I say. "But what if we're meant to be? What if Holly and I are great together and she's the happiest she'll ever be? And what if we don't take this chance because you're worried about something that will never happen?"

Gwen nods. "That's a possibility too."

"So, will you help me?"

Gwen sits for a while, thinking. The silence is killing me, but then she finally says, "Okay, I'll do it."

"You'll do it!" I say. "Thank you, Gwennie." I sweep her up in a hug.

She laughs but then turns serious again. "I'm okay with you liking her," she says. "But don't push anything. You let her decide what she wants."

"I promise."

"If she has feelings for you too—"

"I'm almost positive of that," I say.

She stares me down again before continuing. "As I was saying, if she has feelings for you too, I will fully support it. I know you are a good guy. Plus, I know that you know I will make your life a nightmare, and I'm positive Trent will too, if you ever do anything to hurt her."

"Thank you," I say, my heart brimming with hope.

"I love you, bro, please don't make me hate you." Gwen says, standing and heading up the stairs.

"Good night, sis, sleep well," I say sincerely. I can't believe Gwen is on board!

She turns to look back at me. "Good night, Greg. Don't mess this up."

I swallow. That might be even harder than convincing Gwen to give me a chance with Holly.

CHAPTER 17
Holly

Waking the next morning, I'm still torn between Maverick and Greg. I don't know if I should be back with Maverick or see if there's something more there with Greg. It feels like so much has happened since I arrived at the cabin, and I need to talk with Gwen. She's always been good at parsing through my thoughts with me.

My heart stops. Gwen. She saw us outside in the snow last night. I definitely need to talk to her before this goes from bad to worse. Looking at my clock, it's already nine in the morning. I'm surprised that she hasn't woken me up yet to talk about it. I grab my phone off the charger and text her.

> **Me:** *Hey G, you up?*

She replies almost instantly.

> **Gwen:** *Yep.*

> **Me:** *Good I am going to grab some coffee and then I want to talk with you. I'll meet you in your room in about 10 minutes, ok?*

> **Gwen:** *Ok.*

I bite my lip at her short responses. I'm going to need to make an extra strong cup of coffee.

I walk up the stairs with a coffee for Gwen and a hot cocoa for me, then I slowly open Gwen's door.

"Imagine my surprise when I saw you and Greg outside last night," she says, not even waiting for me to hand her the coffee.

"I know. I'm sorry. I should have talked to you about it last night," I say, handing her the mug.

"Yeah, you should have," she says then takes a gulp.

I sip my hot cocoa. "It's just that I got these texts from Maverick, and then I went to see him."

"You what!" Gwen says after spurting coffee from her mouth.

"Last night, I went to his cabin to talk," I confess, not lifting my eyes to meet her gaze.

"Why would you do that? I thought we were done with that D-bag."

"Well, he apologized to me and says he wants to get back together."

"That isn't a good thing," she huffs out. "I really don't think you should be with Maverick. He's a jerk and has never treated you the way you deserve."

"People can change," I offer half-heartedly.

"Not people like him and not that much. Please do not get back together with him. That would be the absolute worst."

"I don't know what I'm feeling."

"Do you have feelings for my brother?" Gwen asks.

My head snaps up at her blunt question. "I don't know what's going on there," I say truthfully.

"Well, from what I saw last night, I could spell some things out for you."

My cheeks turn red. "Um, yeah, I guess some things between Greg and I have changed."

"Go on," Gwen says.

"Well, there's been this chemistry between us. And we might have kissed."

"What!" says Gwen, almost spilling her coffee. "When did that happen?"

"Before you and Trent got here." I hand her a napkin just in case.

"Okay," she says. "I had no idea about that."

"I know. I wasn't ready to tell you. There's just been a lot going on with Maverick, and I'm just not sure how Greg plays into all of that."

"Look," says Gwen, "if you want to pursue things with my brother, I'm okay with that."

"Really?" I ask, looking up at her. I'm surprised she's taking this so well. I thought she would be exploding right now. But I am absolutely fine with how this is turning out.

"Yes," Gwen says. "I'm just worried that if things go wrong, it could cause a strain in our relationship."

"Nothing would hurt our friendship," I say, pulling Gwen into a hug. "You're like a sister to me. I would never let anything come between us."

"Same," Gwen says.

"I can't promise things would be the same as they are now if something did happen between Greg and me. But I don't know if Greg and I are even going to happen. I can't figure that out until I sort out my relationship with Maverick."

"Or lack thereof," Gwen says.

I sigh. "We've been together for years, G. Should I pretend that doesn't mean something?"

"Hol, you do not want to be with a guy like that. I don't want you to be with a guy like that, not for another year, not for another second."

"But we used to be so good together." I take a sip of my cocoa.

"I can't make this decision for you, but you know where I stand. And I'm not the only one that thinks you're better off without him."

I nod. "Thanks for always being there for me, G."

"I always will be," she says.

We talk for hours before Gwen asks, "You hungry?"

I perk up. "Starving."

"Lunch break it is then," Gwen says. We head downstairs, and Gwen makes another steaming cup of coffee.

I walk over to the fridge then glance inside before moving to the pantry and grabbing a few items.

"How about pizza?" I ask, excitement building inside me at the chance to bake again.

"We don't have pizza dough," she replies from her perch on the counter.

"No worries, I know a good recipe. Are you up for a little cooking lesson?"

"I thought your specialty was baking?" says Greg. I twirl around to see Greg and Trent walking into the kitchen and taking seats at the island.

"Yeah, but you bake the pizza dough, so it's sort of baking, right?" I reply.

I smile up at Greg, my arms full of the ingredients.

He comes over to help me lay everything on the counter. My breath catches when his hands graze my arms. I shake it off, heading over to the fridge to grab the rest of the items we need.

After setting everything out, I look over to Gwen, who is furiously typing away on her phone, coffee left forgotten.

"Everything okay, G?" I ask with concern.

"Ugh, no. It's this new assistant. She does not have the backbone to deal with the vendors, and they are running all over her. I'm sorry, Hol, but I'm gonna need to take care of this."

"No worries," I say cheerily. "I'll get started, and you can help when you get back."

"Okay, but Greg, Trent, help Holly while I deal with this." She types on her phone and then pauses. Looking back at Trent and Greg, she points at them. "And you two, don't mess anything up." Then she's back on her phone and out of the kitchen.

I wash my hands at the sink and take the towel Greg offers me. He walks to a drawer and pulls out three aprons. He slides one over my head as I put the towel back in its place.

"Thanks," I say, taking a look at the words written on the front of my apron. "Bake it 'til you make it." The phrase makes me giggle. "Cute. I love it."

Greg offers an apron to Trent as well, but Trent shakes his head. "You heard Gwen. She said don't mess anything up. I think I will leave the baking up to you two." Instead, Trent gets down a mug and helps himself to some coffee.

"Suit yourself," Greg says. Turning to me, he asks, "What do you think about my apron?"

It reads: "Enter at your own whisk." I break out in giggles from the corniness of the aprons.

"Mom loves this kind of stuff," Greg comments.

"Oh gosh, I forgot how corny your parents can be."

"Yeah, it was annoying growing up, but I appreciate it more now."

I stifle a laugh then focus on the pizza.

"Okay, let's get cooking." I preheat the oven. Then I grab the flour, instant yeast, sugar, and salt and measure and pour them into a bowl.

"You all like garlic?" I ask.

Greg nods.

"Sure do!" says Trent before taking a sip of his coffee. "'Can't have too much garlic' has always been my motto."

"Good. Okay then, Greg, can you grab the garlic powder from the counter and pour some in? I like to flavor my pizza dough. I feel like it gives it a little something, you know?"

"Can't say I do, but I'm here to learn from the master."

"Ha, I wouldn't call myself a master, but you'll see how delicious it is. The garlic powder gives it the perfect touch."

Adding the olive oil and warm water, I stir the mixture with a wooden spoon that has "Stir it, Stir it real good" engraved into the handle. Chuckling, I shake my head.

"What?" Greg asks.

I hold up the handle, and we immediately burst into laughter.

"You two just keep cracking yourselves up, don't you?" Trent teases.

I try unsuccessfully to calm myself and get back to cooking, but every time I look over at Greg, I laugh all over again. It takes us a few minutes to get back under control, stomachs hurting from all the laughter.

"Okay, oh gosh, there better not be any other corny phrases around here," I say. "I might not be able to get this pizza made."

"We can't have that," Trent says.

"No, no we can't." I laugh. "Here." I motion to Greg. "Grab another cup of flour and put it in this bowl."

"As you wish," he replies.

"Okay, now take the bowl over there and cover the inside with olive oil."

Greg does as I instruct then sets the bowl next to me. I reach for the flour and add a dusting to my hand. I gently roll the dough in the bowl until it's fully coated with oil.

A buzz sounds from my phone. I wipe my hands on my apron and check my messages. More texts from Maverick.

> **Maverick:** *Hi Sweetie, I just wanted to check in, have you thought about what we talked about?*

> **Maverick:** *Let me know what you're thinking Sweetie. Are you ready to try harder and make what we have work? Trust has to go both ways, right?*

I take a moment to look at the messages, then turn it off without responding. I am not ready to talk to Maverick. After my chat with Gwen this morning, I just need more time to think things through.

"Everything okay?" Greg asks.

"Yeah," I say. "Let's just get back to the pizzas."

"Let's get those pizzas cooking," says Trent, rubbing his hands together. "I am literally dying of hunger over here." Trent sinks in his barstool to emphasize his point.

"We can't have that," I say then wash my hands at the sink. "Greg, would you pour some flour on the counter here?"

Greg grabs the flour and pours it out too fast. A cloud of white dust puffs up around me. I cough and wave my arms trying to clear the air.

"Oops, sorry," Greg grins.

"You did that on purpose!" I say, eyeing him. "Oh, just you wait, Gregory Kenton."

Trent laughs. "You look like a ghost. If you got it, haunt it."

Greg and I look at each other and then at Trent, who has cracked himself up at his bad pun. We both give a small chuckle and shake our heads at him.

"What?" Trent says. "That was hilarious. You two are just party poopers."

"Right, well, this party pooper wants to eat," I say, "so if you're not going to help, just sit there and look pretty."

Trent rolls his eyes and continues drinking his coffee.

I check on the dough as my phone rings. Maverick again. I silence the call.

The dough has risen as expected and is ready to be kneaded. I deflate the dough and transfer it to the floured surface. I grab some flour to lightly coat my hands, then quickly tag Greg on the cheek with it.

"What the . . ." he stammers before regaining his composure. Then he grabs a pinch of the flour and tosses it at me.

"Hey!" I yell. "Not fair."

"What do you mean not fair? You started it." He laughs, his eyes crinkling as he grabs another pinch of flour and tosses it at me.

"I most definitely did not." I swipe some flour on the tip of his nose. "You're the one who hit me with a cloud of flour."

He swats at my hand then reaches for more flour.

"That was an accident. Yours was intentional," he replies.

"Well, you deserve it." I say.

"Umm, I know I'm no expert," Trent says, "but this looks messier than the cooks at the Pizza Kitchen."

"Hush up, Trent," I say, "or I'll send some of this your way too." I giggle at the flour flying all over the place. We're making a big mess, but it's exhilarating.

I swat at Greg again, leaving a flour handprint on his dark blue shirt.

His eyes narrow playfully before he wipes flour on my arm. "You're having a lot of fun with this, aren't you?" Greg asks me.

"I have to have some fun in life," I say. "It's not like I am living a fairy tale."

Greg stills and rests his hand on my arm. "You'll have a happily ever after, Holly," he says.

His tone is serious. And my stomach fills with butter-flies hearing him use my first name. To him, I've always just been "Palmer," but I guess that's changed. And I'm not sure why. But I don't mind. I could get used to "Holly" coming from his lips. In fact, I prefer it.

I press a hand to my abdomen, trying to calm my stomach. Then I bump Greg with my hip. "Let's knead this dough and get it in the oven."

"Seriously?" Gwen says, walking into the kitchen. An incredulous look shows on her face. "I can't leave you alone for two minutes!"

"I mean, it was more than two minutes," Trent says. "We had to let the dough rise for thirty."

Gwen whips around to Trent, throwing daggers at him with her gaze. "Not. Funny."

Trent holds his hands up. "Okay, I get it. Stop the death stare."

"Sorry," Gwen says, "I just had to deal with a huge mess and didn't expect to walk into one here too." She sighs and pulls out a barstool next to Trent.

"No worries, Gwennie," Greg says. "We'll clean this one up. You just take a break."

I finish rolling out the dough, then spread oil over the top, poking holes with a fork and placing it on the pizza stone.

"Time for toppings," I say. "What are you all in the mood for?"

"Pepperoni, for sure!" says Trent, jumping up and placing pepperonis on the pizza closest to him.

"Sounds good to me," says Gwen, sounding a little calmer.

"What about this one?" I ask Greg, gesturing to the pizza in front of us.

"It's your pizza," Greg says, "so you pick."

"Let's use ham, pineapple, and black olives."

"Hawaiian?" Greg asks, reaching an arm around my back to grab the olives on the other side.

"Yep, it's my favorite!" I say. "And, as you said, my pizza, my toppings."

Greg nudges the olives toward me, but doesn't move his arm, leaving me nestled into the crook of his body. "That I did," he says, leaning over me and smiling.

My body pulsates next to his. I can't help but inhale his smoky cinnamon scent. How do I fit so perfectly next to him? I want to pull him closer and closer to me.

Instead, I grab the olives and smile up at him.

CHAPTER 18
Greg

"That was delicious," Gwen says after finishing her last slice of pizza.

Trent lets out a groan as he lies on the couch. "I think I'll burst if I eat another slice," he says, "but it might be worth it."

"Thank you," says Holly from her spot on the couch next to me.

We're gathered around the fireplace, and I can't help but wish this vacation were longer. Weeks longer. I can't believe I only have six more days left of being with Holly. After this, who knows when we'll be cooking together or when she'll be sidled up next to me again? Knowing that I'll be moving back to Chessie Valley gives me hope. Maybe these interactions won't be as few and as far between as they have been.

Holly's phone buzzes.

She looks down at it and confusion crosses her face.

"Who is it?" asks Gwen.

"Not sure," Holly says. "I don't have this number saved."

She slides her phone open and holds it to her ear. "Hello?" she says tentatively.

"Why aren't you replying to my messages or answering my calls?" comes Maverick's voice loudly over the line.

"Oh, hi," Holly says, jostling the phone. "I just . . . I just needed—"

"You just what, Holly," Maverick says.

My neck tightens. Why is he calling her? I thought he broke up with her. I thought they were over.

"I thought after seeing me last night," says Maverick, "that you'd know how much you want us, how much you need me."

What is he talking about? When did Holly see Maverick? Not last night. I think about making snow angels and Holly falling on top of me and feeling so much chemistry around us and almost kissing.

She wouldn't have seen Maverick after that, would she?

And then I think about Gwen looking at us through her window and how shocked we had been. And Holly and I went our separate ways. Would she have wanted to talk to Maverick after that? Why?

"If we're getting back together," Maverick says, "this is not the way to gain my trust again."

"I—" Holly starts.

Getting back together? Does she want to be with him? My face goes hot with anger.

Gwen and Trent both glance my way, but I ignore them. I thought Holly was beginning to feel something for me. For us.

"I thought you cared about us," says Maverick, echoing my own thoughts. "I thought we were past all the lies and deceit. You've lost your mind if you think I can trust you after you ignore my calls."

"But, I have, I've—" Holly tries again, and tears pool in her eyes.

"But you what? You've got to do better than this."

I'm confused and hurt. Have I been reading all the signs wrong? Her smiles, the flirting, our kiss. Can Holly not feel what is happening between us? Am I just some dumb love-sick guy that wants this to happen so much that I can't see how she actually feels?

"We already know I can't trust you," Maverick says, "and you're going to have to work hard to gain that trust back if you want us to work. I can't—"

Gwen stands, crosses the room, and takes the phone from Holly. Then she hangs up on Maverick.

"What a D-bag!" Gwen says. "You can't seriously still be considering getting back with him."

A tear slips down Holly's face. She looks at her hands.

Trent looks furious. "Holly, why are you letting some guy talk to you like that? Surely you think more of yourself than that!"

Holly flinches at his words.

How can she possibly want to get back together with Maverick? Can't she tell that he's a horrible person? That she deserves so much better? I'm about to say as much when I look at Holly sitting beside me.

She looks so small and broken. Tears slip down her face. The anger in me subsides as my compassion slowly takes over. Throwing questions at her is clearly not helping. And adding more anger on top of Maverick's won't do anything.

I realize that I'm feeling angry for the same reason Maverick is—we both want to be with Holly. Seeing a glimpse of Maverick in me makes me feel horrible. I need to snap out of this. It's not about me and what I want. Holly never asked me to like her. She never asked me to pursue her on this vacation. And what am I doing? Feeling angry that she doesn't want me while she's trying to figure out her relationship with a man she's been with for years.

Taking a deep breath, I turn to Holly. "Holly," I say softly, placing a gentle hand on her arm.

She looks up at me, and another tear falls down her cheek. Damn, that does me in. I hate seeing her full of sadness. I want her to be happy. She deserves that.

"Holly, it's okay," I say. "It isn't and never was your fault. Trent and Gwen mean well. We just care about you and want what's best for you."

"I'm so sorry," says Gwen, pulling Holly into a hug. "I didn't mean to snap at you. I just really don't like Maverick."

"I'm sorry too," says Trent. "But you do deserve better. No guy should ever treat you like that."

"We don't want to see you go back to that toxic relationship," says Gwen.

"You're such a beautiful person," I tell Holly, "inside and out. You need, no, you deserve someone who is going to cherish you."

"Thanks, Greg," Holly says, wiping tears from her cheeks. "I know you all mean well."

"We do," says Trent.

"We love you," says Gwen.

"What can we do to help?" I ask.

"I just want to be happy again. I don't know what to do about Maverick, I don't have much passion for my job, and life just seems so off lately."

"If I can be blunt," says Trent, "I think you need a fresh start."

"What do you mean?" Holly asks.

"Ditch the terrible boyfriend," says Trent. "Quit your job. Find you again."

Trent's right. She does need to focus on herself. She's been dragged down by Maverick for so many years. She needs to follow her own dreams and passions. How selfish have I been to think that my feelings for her were more important than her own self-worth?

"You make it sound so simple," Holly says.

"We'll help you," I say, squeezing her hand.

Holly nods. "You're right. I need to focus on me and what makes me happy."

"That's right, girl!" says Gwen.

"But I can't just up and quit my job," Holly says. "What would I do?"

I chuckle because I know exactly what she should do. "This is just my opinion," I say, "but I think you should open a bakery."

"Whoa!" says Trent.

Holly looks up at me in shock.

"Holly, you love baking, don't you?" I ask.

"Yes."

"You have a real talent for it."

"That's for sure," says Trent.

"You know the three of us would order from you," I continue, "and when word gets out, people will be knocking your door down to get your delicious pastries and whatnot."

Gwen looks excitedly at Holly. "You always said you wanted to open a bakery."

"I mean, yeah," Holly says and lets out a breath. "I did when I was a kid. But I can't just quit my job and open a bakery. I have bills to pay, you know."

"Sure you can," Gwen says. "How do you think I got my event-planning business up and running?"

"Well, that's you. I'm me. I have to know there will be reliable income. And there's so much I'd have to do before I could even make a penny. I'd need a name, a website, a location, business cards, and so much more. I can't even think of that right now."

"Well, I could help with the business cards and website," I tell her.

"Really?" she says, beaming at me. "Thanks, Kenton."

"And you wouldn't have to have a storefront at first," I continue. "Just get your client base up as you work from your home. Then you could write off part of your rent as a work expense as well."

"That sounds great," Holly says. "But who's going to want to hire a baker who didn't even go through culinary school?"

"Oh, that's easy," says Gwen. We all turn to her, waiting for her to continue. "What?" Gwen says. "Is it not obvious to anyone else?"

"Nope, just you, Gwennie," I say.

"Well, me, duh," Gwen says.

"We still don't get it," I say.

"My clients are forever asking for recommendations on bakers and caterers," says Gwen. "I will add you to my vendor list and always mention your bakery first. It will take one of the decision-making pieces off my clients and give Holly instant business. It may not be opening up a storefront, but it would give you the jumpstart to save up for it."

"Are, are you serious, G?" Holly asks, her eyes shining with the last of her unshed tears.

"Of course I am. I wouldn't say it if I wasn't. You're my best friend, but more than that, I know your skills. You've got talent that you are wasting. Take that pizza, for example. It's at a professional level!"

Startling us all, Holly leaps out of her seat to hug Gwen, almost knocking over Gwen and Gwen's chair. "Thank you, thank you, thank you. You won't regret this!"

"And Kenton," she says, turning to me with her eyes sparkling. "Thank you for suggesting this."

"Of course," I say. "You have an amazing talent. You should go for it."

A smile breaks across her face, and she wraps her arms around me.

Her closeness causes my body to immediately react. My pulse races. Holly is hugging me. Of her own free will. Her arms wrap around my neck, her touch making my stomach do flips. We are cheek to cheek. Her hair presses up against my face, and the delicious vanilla-coconut scent puts me in a trance, causing my breath to hitch. I turn and face her as she pulls back, still smiling.

Heat radiates through my chest. All that matters is that she is happy. Of course, I'd love to be the one to make her happy for the rest of her life.

Wow. . . . Too soon. Way too soon for that kind of talk. I mean, I've known Holly for about thirteen years and have had a crush on her for as long. I'm so over just being friends with Holly. But I know that right now she needs to focus on herself. And I'm okay with that. I'll support her every step of the way. And maybe after that, maybe then it will be my turn to pursue Holly.

"I'd be happy to sample anything you make," Trent says. "For marketing purposes of course."

Holly laughs and embraces Trent too.

"Deal!" she exclaims.

"We can get started on it while we're here," Gwen says. "You can use any of the supplies Mom and Dad have here to bake whatever your heart desires."

"Oh my gosh. I'm so excited!" Holly says. "I don't think I've been this excited about anything in forever."

"I'm glad you're happy, Palmer," I say. "You deserve to be."

"Thank you, Kenton," she says. "I would've been a mess without you these past few days. But instead, you've kept Murphy at bay and been the best."

"I am so freaking excited," says Gwen, "that you are going to not only be baking again but practically working with me. Call me selfish, but I have missed you, and now I'll get to see you all the time!"

"I'm excited too, G," says Holly.

"To mark this momentous occasion, let's go shopping tomorrow. You'll need to get something to remember the day you decided to focus on you."

"I would love that," Holly says.

"And before we begin any business prep," Gwen says gesturing to the disaster we left in the kitchen, "that is going to need to be taken care of."

"Oof," says Trent, peeking into the kitchen. "How did you get flour on the ceiling?" "You two," Gwen says, pointing to Holly and me. "You will be cleaning up your mess. I am going to take a bubble bath."

"Okay, okay," I say, "we know, we made the mess, we'll clean it up."

"You're right," says Holly. "Go relax. We've got this."

Gwen nods and heads up the stairs.

"I'm going to head up to my room," says Trent, winking at me.

I guess I owe Trent one now.

We spend the next hour cleaning the dishes, scrubbing the walls, and mopping the floor. By the time we're done, I'm not only physically exhausted but emotionally drained too. Listening to Maverick's phone call and realizing I need to give Holly more space has taken its toll. Not to mention the life-changing events that have happened in such a short time. I'm moving home. And now Holly's going to open a bakery. Before I came on this trip, I never could have imagined how this would end up.

"Well, I'm going to head on up to bed," I tell Holly. "It's going to be a fun-filled day tomorrow for you. I think Trent and I will probably hit the slopes while you and Gwen are shopping."

"I'm worn out too," Holly says.

We're silent as we walk through the house turning off lights and locking the doors.

When we reach the top of the stairs, Holly wraps her arms around me.

"Thank you," she says. "For everything." Her green eyes gleam in the moonlight coming in through the hall window.

Another hug? A guy can get used to this.

Arms around me, she rests her head on my chest, and I lean my head against hers. She fits perfectly in my arms. Like our bodies were made specifically for each other. "Of course," I say. "I hope you know I'd do anything for you."

"I know you would," she says, wrapping her arms tighter around me.

I look into her face. Her eyes fill, joy cascading off her. I want to pull her closer to me. I want her lips on mine. I want to tell her everything I'm feeling. But I can't. Not now. Having her this close but out of reach at the same time is too much for me. I swallow a lump in my throat.

"Good night, Palmer," I say, hoping this hug will never end and at the same time hoping that it will so I can be put out of my misery.

"Thank you again for everything," she says. Then she pulls away and walks to her door.

She pushes it open but stops, turning back to me. "Greg?" she asks.

"Yes?"

She waits a beat then takes two steps over to me, placing one hand on my chest. She raises up on her toes and then presses her lips against mine.

I'm frozen in place, my lips on fire. What is happening? I thought she wanted to focus on herself. I thought I was going too fast. What does this mean? Does this mean she does want me and not Maverick? Is this her way of telling me she's ready for me to pursue her?

I wasn't planning on kissing her. I don't want to take away from the steps she's made to live for herself by sharing my feelings. Do I want to tell her everything? Yes, yes I do. Am I ecstatic that she finally decided to end things with Maverick and think of herself? Of course. Now I actually have a shot with her. Well, at least I hope I do. If this kiss is telling me anything, I think I might be right.

She kisses me harder, deeper. A wave of heat courses through my body, causing my heart to skip multiple beats. *Don't be an idiot, Greg. The girl you've been obsessed with is kissing you. Kiss her back!*

Bending down, I brush back her hair. Matching her intensity, I press my lips against hers.

I let myself live in this moment. I take her waist in my hand. She reaches up and wraps her hands around my neck, fingers dancing through my hair. The press of our bodies coaxes a small moan from her.

Deepening our kiss, pure pleasure runs through me.

Her lips are warm and soft against mine, another moan escaping her. She parts them slightly, allowing my tongue to slip inside. As our tongues intertwine, her kiss grows forceful, and she draws my lip between her tongue and teeth. Passion floods through me.

She lets out a frustrated moan as she tries to press tighter against me.

I do the same.

My need for her rising, I pick her up, and she wraps her legs around my waist. I hold her and devour her mouth with mine. Holly does the same to me.

We stay this way, tasting, feeling, enjoying each other's kisses until we hear shuffling coming from one of the bedrooms. Remembering that we're not alone, we slowly break apart.

"Sleep well," Holly says, her eyes full of fire and her lips swollen as she lowers down. Her hand lingers on my chest a moment before she turns, walks in her room, and slowly closes the door.

My hand reaches up to touch the place her lips seared my skin, and I stand frozen to the spot.

Holly just kissed me.

She.

Kissed.

Me.

Me!

I whisper, "Sleep well, Holly," and head to my room.

CHAPTER 19

Holly

I close my door, leaning against it for support. I just kissed Greg. Again. A wide smile spreads across my face just thinking about it. The instant my lips touched his skin, I felt that now familiar flicker. I hadn't intended to kiss him at first. I just wanted to show my thanks with a hug, but when we broke away, I don't know what it was. I can't even explain it. A hug just wasn't enough.

He was so wonderful today. He saw me. When I couldn't answer Gwen's and Trent's questions, he noticed I was feeling down. His kind words, his comforting touch. Knowing what I'd wanted, what I needed, but not telling me what to do. Letting me come to it on my own. He really saw me. My heart feels so full.

Greg has been so wonderful, so amazing, never expecting anything from me in return. So I kissed him, trying to tell him with that kiss everything I couldn't verbalize.

I had never done that with Maverick before. I never had a kiss hold so much meaning and emotion. And I know I'll never share a kiss like that with Maverick. He was a real jerk to me on the phone. Everyone is right. I deserve so much more than him.

I am so done with Maverick.

I deserve someone who respects me and would never speak to me the way Maverick has. Someone who cares about me and causes electric sparks to jolt through me. Someone who makes my toes curl. Someone who sees more in me than I even see in myself. Someone like Greg.

Oh boy, there's no denying it now.

There's something between me and Greg.

My mind reels as I put on my pajamas and slip into bed. But are the feelings I have for Greg worth pursuing? Is it worth potentially ruining our friendship? Am I moving too fast? Maverick and I just broke up days ago. Should I already be feeling this way toward someone else? I don't know. The only thing I do know is that I am definitely falling for Greg.

I wake up early the next morning and make a batch of muffins. When the boys come down, Greg smiles at me, and I beam back at him.

Trent grabs two muffins, and Greg helps himself to one as well.

"Gwen still asleep?" Greg asks.

"Must be," I say. "You boys going to be out all day?"

"That's the plan," says Trent and takes a bite of a muffin.

"Have fun," I say, disappointed that I won't be seeing Greg for most of the day.

"Want to meet up at the diner for lunch?" Greg asks.

"Oh! The diner," says Trent, "that'll bring back some good memories."

Laughing, I nod. "That sounds great."

Greg can't stop smiling, and I can't stop smiling at him. Relief fills me now that I know I'll see him in just a few hours.

Greg waves as he and Trent slip out the door ready for the slopes.

Gwen joins me a little while later. I already have coffee and a muffin ready for her at the breakfast nook. We sit and eat together in companionable silence. Almost a lifetime of friendship has taught me to know better than to try talking to Gwen before she's had the right dose of coffee in the morning.

Once the coffee has enough time to seep into her bloodstream and make it through her body a hundred times, I decide now is as good a time as any to let her know what I decided last night.

"G?" I ask.

"What?" she mumbles.

"I wanted to let you know that I decided to end things with Maverick—for good this time."

Gwen jumps to her feet, nearly knocking her now-empty mug to the ground. "Why didn't you tell me that three coffees ago?" she says.

I laugh. "I just didn't want to mess with your morning routine."

She wraps me in a hug. "Finally!" she says. "I'm so glad you're choosing you."

"Me too," I say.

"Now we definitely need to go shopping to mark this occasion," Gwen says, already grabbing her purse. "And lunch is on me. Hell, anything you want is on me. I'm just so happy for you."

I laugh, and soon we're out the door, hitting the town— well village, but who cares about semantics. This may be a little ski village, but it has some of the best shopping in the area.

Gwen's so excited and pumped, she's a chatterbox the whole walk to the village.

We go into probably every store, trying on tons of outfits. I end up with a few items, but Gwen gets almost triple the amount I do. She loves to shop. I don't know how she can afford all of it. Maybe her event-planning business is going better than I thought. Well, that's good for me, right?

Stopping at a bakery in the village, we pick up some celebratory cookies.

"Just think," says Gwen, gesturing around the bakery. "One day, this is going to be you."

I smile. "All thanks to you and the boys."

"But mainly me, right?" Gwen says and winks.

I laugh. "Yes, mainly you, G."

We pay for our baked goods and leave the bakery.

As I bite into a slice of a maple-glazed brioche loaf, Gwen asks, "Has anything caught your eye?"

"Yeah," I say, holding up a few of my shopping bags.

"No," she says, "I mean something that you can buy to celebrate you picking you. Opening a bakery, ending things with Maverick, choosing you."

When she lists it all out like that, it sounds like my entire life has been changed around since coming to Snowden—and I guess it has. She's right. I do need something to remember this by.

"I'm still looking," I tell her.

After a few more shops, we find a small little boutique and head in. I look around the jewelry section. There are beautiful bracelets and sparkly earrings, but nothing speaks to me. Nothing calls to me.

I don't wear much jewelry normally, having only a few pieces that mean something to me. A pair of earrings from my parents when I graduated high school. A bracelet from my grandmother when I turned sixteen. So if I do get a piece of jewelry, it has to do more than catch my eye. It has to mean something.

"Can I help you find something, dear?" A woman comes over to the jewelry counter.

"I'm not quite sure what I'm looking for, actually," I say.

"Well, I'm June," she says. "I own the shop, so I know every piece of jewelry by heart. Are you looking for an everyday piece or something flashy?"

"I want something that speaks to me." I say. "I've just made some pretty big life changes. This moment in my life feels significant. I want to find the perfect piece for it. Something that says I am moving on from where I've been and toward better things." I don't know why I'm opening up so much to this woman, but the more I share, the more empowered I feel about the decisions I've made.

"I understand," says June. "Every woman should own a piece of jewelry that speaks to her like that."

I'm nearly finished looking over the jewelry in the case when my eye catches on a dainty necklace.

"Can I see that one?" I ask June.

"Such a pretty piece," she says, handing it over to me to examine. The necklace has a dainty rose gold flower with a stone in the bottom center.

"What is the stone?" I ask.

"That is a rainbow moonstone," says June. "It's said to bring balance, harmony, and hope while enhancing creativity and inner confidence." June touches the stone in the center of the flower. "It's paired with the lotus, which is such an interesting flower. Even though it comes from muddy waters, it blooms without blemishes. It symbolizes a strength to move past your barriers and rise above it all."

My eyes fill with tears. This is perfect. I can rise above my past and come out stronger than ever.

"It sounds like exactly what you were looking for," June says, smiling with me.

I nod. "I'll take it."

"Hol, let me see what you found," Gwen comes up from behind me.

We ooh and aah over the necklace as June tells Gwen about the lotus flower and the rainbow moonstone. We both agree this is the perfect piece for me.

"Do you have a little stand or something I could set it on?" I ask June. "When I'm not wearing it, I want to keep it on display. I like to keep my important trinkets on a bookshelf to remind myself of special moments in my life."

June smiles and grabs a delicate stand behind her. "That sounds wonderful, dear."

Gwen squeezes my arm. "It will look perfect next to the snow globe you got on our trip to Ireland or the baseball from the Sounds game."

"It will," I say.

June wraps up the stand, and I wear the necklace out of the shop.

After a whirlwind morning of shopping, we are starving.

"Can't wait to go to the diner," says Gwen.

"Me either," I say. "It's been a while."

"Split the cheesy fries with me?"

"Always," I say, linking my arm through hers.

Soon, we're settled in a booth at Snowden Diner, waiting for Trent and Greg. I have a peppermint hot chocolate and Gwen a coffee. A mountain of fries covered in cheese sits between us.

"The boys are definitely going to need to help us finish this one," I say.

"You think?" Gwen says, grabbing a fry. "I might be able to eat this whole thing." But before it reaches her lips, she stops, and her face darkens.

"What is it?" I ask.

"Hol, listen to me," says Gwen. "Don't look out your window, okay."

"What? Why?" I ask, now itching to turn and look.

"It's the D-bag."

"Maverick!" I say in a hushed whisper, clutching at my necklace.

"He's walking past the diner. Hopefully, he will just keep going and not even see us."

My skin prickles on the back of my neck just thinking about him being a few feet from me. Seriously, Murphy? Can't a girl enjoy a day out without running into her ex? I take deep breaths trying to calm myself.

I know I don't have feelings for him anymore. But I also know that I have to tell Maverick that we are in fact officially over. I know he'll just keep calling and texting until I do.

I trace my finger over the lotus, remembering how far I've come and that I've chosen me. The necklace's symbolism gives me the strength I need to confront Maverick. I turn and look out the window. And there he is.

But he's not alone. He's walking arm in arm with a woman, the same woman I ran into outside his cabin. What is she doing with him?

Then Maverick turns and meets my gaze. As soon as he realizes it's me, he fumes and his jaw clenches, but I don't drop my gaze.

Maverick storms into the restaurant, leaving the woman in the red coat on the sidewalk looking perplexed. As he reaches our table, he says, "I can't believe you, Holly! I'm being so kind, letting you have a second chance with me. And you decide to hang up on me??"

"She didn't hang up on you, I did," says Gwen, standing up and putting her arms on her hips as she stares him down. "You were a jerk, and I wasn't about to let her take that crap from you. She deserves better."

Just then, the door to the diner opens and Greg and Trent walk in. Like magnets drawn to each other, my eyes meet with Greg's and he smiles. Then, he notices the look on my face. Immediately, he spots Maverick and makes a beeline toward us.

"I'm not talking to you," Maverick says, practically spitting at Gwen.

"Watch it, Maverick," says Greg in a steady yet icy tone.

"I don't have to watch anything," Maverick says through gritted teeth. I'm here to talk to my girlfriend, so you should butt out."

"I think you should back off," says Trent.

"Is that a threat?" says Maverick heatedly.

Greg just shrugs. "Your words, not ours."

"Honestly, if it comes down to you and us," says Trent, "I promise you, we will win."

Maverick takes in the size of both Greg and Trent, who are inches taller than him. It takes a beat, but Maverick realizes his lanky stature would do nothing against Greg and Trent. He looks over at me, eyes so wide I can see the whites almost bulging with his anger.

Standing, I place my hand lightly on Greg's and Trent's arms. "Thank you," I say. "I've got it from here." I step forward, facing Maverick. "I deserve better than you. I deserve someone who is going to respect and honor our relationship, someone who treats me with kindness and makes me feel beautiful. And you, you are not that person."

Just then the woman in the red coat walks in. "Everything okay, Mav?" she asks.

"Everything's fine, Carmen," Maverick says shortly. "Why don't you go wait outside?"

Everything hits me at once.

Carmen? His client from the slopes? My head snaps up. I'm seeing red. Literally. The red coat on the slopes. The red coat outside Maverick's cabin. The red lacy bra in his bathroom. The red coat in front of me. I almost laugh at the insanity of it all.

Gwen touches my hand. "You good?"

"Seriously, Maverick?" I say in a steely tone, looking from Carmen to Maverick.

I place my hands on my hips. I am fully channeling Gwen right now. I feel everyone's eyes on me.

"What?" Maverick asks.

"Are you freaking kidding me? I get it now." Venom laces my words. "You've been cheating on me."

"What are you talking about?" Maverick glares at me. I shake my head, not even shocked at this point.

"With her," I say, gesturing to Carmen. "Your supposed client or whatever."

"Maverick," says Carmen, "what is this woman talking about?"

I huff out a laugh. "How long, Maverick? How long have you been cheating on me? No, you know what? I don't want to know. I just want you out of my life forever. I don't ever want to see you again."

"You can't do that, Holly!" Maverick yells, fuming.

"What is going on?" Carmen asks, looking appalled.

"You've strung me along for years, Maverick," I continue. "You've made me feel so small and insecure. You constantly put me second. It's always what you want to do, what will help your career, what is in your best interest."

I grasp my necklace for strength. "You've never cared about me. You made me feel like nothing I did, nothing I could ever do would be good enough. You made me feel worthless. You've made my dreams feel small and insignificant. I put my entire life on hold for you, and not once have you ever given part of your life for mine. And I'm done. I'm choosing me. I'm choosing my life and my dreams. And you're not in them. We are over, Maverick."

Confidence fills me from head to toe.

"Oh, and Carmen," I add, "don't think he will treat you any different. He's a manipulator and a liar. And as of a few days ago, I was his girlfriend, so he's also a cheater."

"Is that true, Maverick?" Carmen asks.

"No, of course not!" Maverick replies.

I shrug. "Don't think that you can change him," I tell Carmen. "He's a D-bag, and you should get as far away from him as you can."

Maverick looks dumbfounded, mouth agape and eyes wide.

Carmen runs out the door.

Maverick turns to me, seething. "You can't do this to me!" He grabs both of my arms tightly, holding me in place.

Within seconds, Greg is in his face.

"I suggest you let her go," says Greg, grabbing Maverick's shoulder.

"Back off," says Trent, looming over Maverick.

"Never call or contact me again," I tell Maverick, pushing him away from me. "We are so done."

Maverick lets go of me and takes a step back.

"Leave," says Trent.

Maverick turns to go but stops. "You were never worth it, Holly," he says. "You'll never be good enough for anyone."

Greg lunges at him.

"Stop!" I say, pulling on Greg's arm.

Maverick runs out the door.

"It's fine," I tell Greg. "I don't care what he thinks."

Then Gwen's arms are around me. "Holy crap, girl," she squeals, "that was amazing. I am so proud of you!"

I shake my head at her, stunned at myself. "I can't believe I just did that."

"You are a rock star, Holly," says Trent.

"You finally gave that D-bag a piece of your mind," says Gwen, her voice full of pride and a huge grin on her face.

"You okay, Holly?" says Greg, glancing first at my arms where Maverick had grabbed hold of me, then to my eyes. His eyes search mine.

"Yes. Thank you for your help—all of you," I say.

"You were the one that made him leave," says Greg. "We just gave you some support."

"Seriously, thank you. You all are the best friends I could ever ask for." My eyes fill with tears as I lock them with Greg's.

What. Just. Happened.

Did I really speak up for myself? Did I actually break up with Maverick for good?

I did.

And now, I'm choosing me.

CHAPTER 20
Greg

I watch as Gwen and Holly leave the diner. I give Holly a smile, happy that Maverick is out of her life. Happy that she stood up for herself. Happy that she's focusing on what makes her happy. Happy that Gwen will be with her for the next little while, at least.

Do I wish it was me comforting and cheering Holly on instead? Yes. Would I have gone shopping all day just to spend more time with her? Of course. Could I stop myself from flirting with her? No. No I couldn't.

"So," says Trent after we make our way back to the slopes, "that was an interesting lunch."

"I can't stand that guy!"

"Same. He's a real jerk. Our Holly is too good for the likes of him."

"She's too good for anyone."

"Hopefully not anyone." Trent grins and jabs my arm.

I laugh and roll my eyes.

"Have you talked to her yet?" he asks as we board the ski lift.

"No, not yet. I almost did, but then Gwen saw us."

"Saw you?"

"It was kind of an intimate moment."

"Dude, that's great!" Trent says. "I mean, not the Gwen seeing it part but the you having moments part. How did Gwen take it?"

"At first, not well, but we talked about it, and I think she is maybe kind of okay with me liking Holly."

"Don't worry about it, dude," Trent says. "It's just new. She'll come around to it."

"Yeah, I hope so," I say. "And there's something else."

"What?" Trent asks.

"Holly kissed me last night."

"What! Dude, that's awesome!" Trent says as he does a little shimmy, slightly shaking the lift as we continue our climb up the mountain.

"I know. It was just, I think we just got caught up in the moment, but still . . . that should mean something, right?"

"Of course it does."

"I hope so, but there was a lot going on that day. Maybe she just let her emotions take over."

Trent folds his arms across his chest. "Seriously dude, get out of your head. She's crazy about you. She's just wary right now because of Jerk-face."

"I'd love for you to be right." I blow out a breath. Could she really be crazy about me? It sounds too good to be true. I don't know.

"Stop it," Trent says, punching me in the shoulder. "Tell her how you feel. I mean, you've had a crush on her for thirteen years!"

"You're right. I'll tell her."

"Good!"

"Thanks for always having my back, man," I say.

"Always do."

"I really am looking forward to working with you at the marina," I tell him. "I want to be more involved, see the benefits from my marketing work."

"You'll definitely get that at the marina. I'm hoping you can help us improve the lineup of events we host. Mom and

Dad have been talking about it for years, but we've just been keeping up managing the current clientele," admits Trent.

"I'll make that my top priority," I say.

We hop off the lift and head over to one of the runs. I'm excited about bringing more to the marina and about being around my friends again. I've been so happy these few days with the four of us at the cabin.

Trent's right about Holly too. I've wasted too many years not telling her how I feel. Before this trip is over, I'll let Holly know exactly how I feel about her—that I want a future with her, a lifetime with her.

The next morning, I walk out in the hallway as Holly comes out of the bathroom fresh from a shower.

"Ready to work on my website?" she asks.

"Yep," I say. "Just going to shower really quick."

"I'll be downstairs," she says, squeezing my arm as she passes by.

I stand there like an idiot, watching Holly walk downstairs and giving her a little wave when she reaches the bottom. She smiles softly and waves back.

Jeez, I'm a dork, and she probably thinks I'm even more of a dork. Why does one look at her take the breath from my lungs? She looks beautiful with her hair pulled up and her sweater showing off her neckline.

Shaking my head, I walk into the bathroom. The room's still steamy from Holly's shower. Thinking of Holly standing naked under the hot water makes my imagination run wild. She makes me want to lasso the moon, tie a bow on it, and surprise her with it.

I can't wait to get downstairs and get going on her bakery business. I don't even care that the whole reason

I went on this trip was to take time away from work. Any chance to spend more time with Holly, and I'm there.

I'm excited about helping her launch her business from scratch. I love marketing, but lately, I've been so focused on the analytics and meeting of numbers that I haven't had a chance to do the work that I love. This will be a good opportunity for me to find my passion again. And the fact that I get to help Holly is the icing on the cake.

Walking downstairs, I can smell the mouthwatering scent of baked goods. It has me imagining walking into Holly's own bakery. This would be the smell people came in for each morning.

I can picture her having one of those small, intimate bakeries with a few tables and chairs scattered around. Families will bring their kids in for special treats. Friends will come and relax there. Brides will beg for her to make their wedding cakes.

Holly would be a beautiful bride.

I rub the back of my neck. Why am I thinking of her as a bride? It's too soon to allow myself to think about that.

I turn my thoughts back to her bakery. Holly will be in a little apron, her hair in her signature messy bun. She'll greet each customer with a warm smile that brightens even the grumpiest person's day. It's shocking how vividly I can picture it all, but I can see the whole thing. Problem is, where am I in this image? Can I become the groom to her bride?

I stop as I approach the kitchen to watch Holly work. She's already baked one batch of muffins and is setting them on the counter to cool. Humming a song, she turns to look at me with a big smile across her face.

"I hope you like cinnamon and oranges," she says.

"If that's what I'm smelling, then I think I *love* cinnamon and oranges," I reply.

I can't help it. Seeing her in her element brings me so much joy. She's a sight to behold. There's no way I can be states away from her after this trip. I'm going to have to move back to Chessie Valley pronto.

Watching her pull another batch of muffins out of the oven, I realize I should have told her years ago how I feel. Why have I wasted so much time? We could've been together for years. We might have been married by now, and she'd never have wasted all those years with Maverick.

I can't mess this up. I'm going to create the most amazing website I've ever created. I'll show her how much she means to me, then I'll tell her how I feel. How I've felt for years.

Holly sets the newest batch on the counter to cool, then she sprinkles something on top.

"What are you adding to the muffins?" I ask, coming up behind her.

"Oh, my aunt always adds sugar to the tops of muffins when we visit her. It's something I always do now when I make muffins too. It gives them a little sweet crunch when you bite into them."

She hands me a muffin to sample. "Here, see for yourself what I mean."

"Shouldn't we wait for Gwen and Trent for breakfast?" I ask.

"No, actually, they stopped through earlier this morning. Gwen has to work today. With the issues the other day, she needs to make sure things go smoothly for her upcoming event. Don't worry, she took up about a gallon of coffee to her room."

"Of course she did," I say and laugh.

"Trent actually came down while you were showering," Holly continues, twirling a loose strand of hair. "He went snowboarding. I told him I'd let you know in case you wanted to join him and do the website stuff later."

Bless you, Gwen and Trent. Now I have the morning alone with Holly.

"No, I'm good. I'm ready to begin on the website when you are."

I peel off the paper lining of my muffin, the cinnamon-orange smell filling my nose. Inhaling the sweet scent, I take a bite, unable to control the moan escaping my lips.

Giggling at me, she reaches over to grab herself a muffin. "So I take it you like them?"

I nod, taking another bite.

"It's delish," I say, my mouth full of the best muffin I've ever tasted.

Swallowing the bite and giving her a goofy grin, I add, "I don't know if anyone's ever told you, but you should go into the baking business."

She grins back at me, eyes crinkling with amusement. "You know," she says, tapping a finger against her cheek, "I think someone may have mentioned that to me once."

"Well, they're brilliant, and you should definitely listen to them."

"I just might do that," she says.

"These should always be on your menu," I say, holding up a half-eaten muffin.

"You don't say?" she laughs.

"I do say."

"You flatter me, Kenton. I'm sure these muffins are good, as Margot always wants me to make them, but are they seriously that good?"

"Umm . . . yes, one thousand percent yes."

I finish my third muffin and watch her add sugar to the next batch. "I could live off these things."

I watch as she mixes more batter and scoops it into the muffin pans. I could watch her all day. She puts the pan into the oven and turns to lean against the counter as she sets the handheld timer. Her gaze catches mine.

Cheeks blushing, she says, "You're staring at me."

I slowly walk toward her, then press my lips to hers. If I thought the cinnamon-orange flavor of the muffins tasted delicious, it was nothing compared to how Holly tasted. I hadn't planned on kissing her, but she looked so lovely, so happy.

She doesn't stiffen at my embrace, but rather she leans into it. I savor her, deepening our kiss as our tongues explore each other. The flavor of the muffins mixing with her natural sweetness has my heart racing. She reaches up to pull me closer, but I step back. We can't get carried away this time, not with her just ending things with Maverick.

The confusion in her eyes has me forgetting all reason. I step toward her once more, tenderly lifting her onto the counter before pulling her up against me.

"Oh!" she giggles, surprised but not upset at our closeness. Her gentle laugh causes my heart to leap. It's the most beautiful sound. I'd do everything in my power to make her smile. I'd do anything to help her see how amazing she is, how much talent she has, how beautiful she is. I have to tell her what she means to me. I have to tell her everything.

"Holly . . ." My voice catches in my throat.

"Shh." She places a finger gently to my lips, her eyes a brilliant green, like gemstones.

She moves her hand to cup my face and pull me in. I slip my hands under her sweater. She shivers slightly as my warm hands gently rub her soft skin.

Fire pulsates throughout my body. I adore her. I long for her. She has no clue how strong my feelings are for her.

I am hers. Always. Forever. I won't let anyone hurt her again. Our breaths are short and quick as we enjoy the taste of each other. The feeling of being in each other's arms.

The timer buzzes, breaking us out of our trance. Leaning my forehead against hers, I kiss her softly on the lips before stepping back and gently lowering her off the counter. She smiles as she turns to check on the muffins.

I am beyond a shadow of a doubt head over heels for Holly. Stepping back, I grab a glass from the cabinet and fill it quickly with ice cold water. Downing the entire glass in one breath, I set it on the counter and clear my throat.

"Come snowshoeing with me tomorrow morning," I say.

"Snowshoeing? Isn't that, like, hiking in the snow with those big snowboard-looking shoes?" She turns toward me, looking adorable with oversized oven mitts on her hands, muffin tin between them.

Her description makes me laugh. "Yes, snowshoes, they aren't necessary but they definitely make things easier. So you're up for it?" I ask, a soft smile on my lips.

"Uh, sure. . . . Why not? Can't be too hard." She carefully takes each muffin out of the tin and sets them on a rack to cool.

"Great! Meet me in the mudroom tomorrow morning, say 6:30 a.m."

Her mouth drops open as she stares at me with an incredulous look on her face, a muffin still in her hand. "6:30 in the morning?"

"Yes, is that okay? It'll just make where we're going so much better."

"Sure. For you, I'll make that work," she says, standing on her tiptoes and kissing me on the cheek. "Where are we going tomorrow?" she asks.

"I can't tell you that," I say, wrapping my arms around her.

The rest of the day is full of baking, stealing kisses, and designing her website. I could relive this day over and over and never tire of it. But as good as today is, I know tomorrow morning, when I tell her how I feel, will be so much better.

CHAPTER 21
Holly

Morning comes quickly. Feeling excited about my adventure with Greg, getting out of bed is the easiest it's been since I've been here. Where is he taking me? What are we doing? I dress in a hurry, putting on my blue winter leggings, a peach sweater, and my lotus necklace. On my way down the stairs, I throw my hair up in my signature messy bun.

Greg's already in the mudroom when I get there, dressed again like he's an outdoor magazine's dream model. With short scruff on his face, he looks rugged and sexy as all hell.

"Morning, Holly," he says. My heart skips a beat as he beams up at me.

"You are way too chipper for how early it is," I say, shaking my head.

"You look pretty awake yourself," he says, slipping on his snowshoes. "Are you ready?"

"Any clues about where we're going?" I ask, sitting down to clip snowshoes on my boots like I'd seen him do.

"Nope, no clues. You'll see soon enough." He holds out his hand to help me up, and we head outside. We take the same trail behind the Kentons' cabin as we had on the first day, but instead of heading right at the fork in the path toward the slopes, we take a left.

Within a few yards, the path opens up to a field of snow.

"I bet this place is full of flowers during the spring," I say.

"It is. Mom and Dad come up here occasionally during the summer, and this area is always full of wildflowers."

"It sounds beautiful."

We're walking side by side through the field. It's still slightly dark outside, but I can tell the sun's on the brink of rising. Soon I'll finally have some light to see by. Though even in the dark, Greg has been a great guide. He knows his way through the forest and field as if he'd done this a thousand times before. In all honesty, he probably has.

"If you like this, wait until you see where we're going," says Greg, grinning at me.

I return the gesture, my eyes sparkling with excitement.

"Just a little farther up this way," he says, "past the next curve, and we'll be there."

We've only been walking for about twenty minutes, but I'm thankful to hear that where we're going isn't too much farther.

Noticing movement in the trees to the left of me, I grab Greg's arm.

He stills, looking first to where I'm holding him then to where I point. A buck and a doe stand together under a snow-covered tree.

"They're so graceful," I whisper.

He smiles and nods.

We stand still, watching them. I am in awe at the beauty of nature and thankful that Greg brought me out here this morning. He is constantly surprising me. We wait until the deer walk farther into the forest before continuing on our way.

Suddenly the field opens up to an even bigger valley. The mountains stand in the distance. Greg steers us to a log. He sits down, patting the spot next to him.

I oblige and sit.

"Watch over that way, just between the two mountain peaks," he says, pointing in front of us.

I nod, taking him in before my gaze turns to where he gestured.

Just a few minutes later as the sun begins to rise, the first beams of light appear.

"Oh!" I gasp. They light up the sky, and it changes from midnight blue to purple, then to pink and reddish orange.

Wanting to experience this moment with Greg, I slide closer to him. Greg lifts his arm around me, pulling me in against him. Immediately, the heat of him begins to warm me, his smoky cinnamon scent overwhelming my senses. I'm no longer cold, no longer tired.

As the sun lights up the world around us, the snow glistens like thousands of diamonds. There's something about this place and the way the sun rises over the mountain peaks that makes me feel serene. But sitting next to Greg and taking this in together, that is what makes me feel breathless.

"This is the most magnificent thing I've ever seen," I say, unable to take my eyes off the view in front of me.

"Yes, it is," he says beside me, his voice catching in his throat.

I smile and turn toward him, immediately blushing at the intensity of his gaze. His hand softly cradles my face, and I glance into his deep brown eyes. His eyes soften with adoration, and he strokes my cheek. Involuntarily, I part my lips, and his eyes immediately lock onto them. My pulse races, and my heartbeat sounds in my ears.

I catch myself leaning in toward Greg. Why am I so affected right now? How does this keep happening? I freeze my lips just inches away from his. Then Greg's lips are on mine, soft and sweet. Not needy like they were the last time we kissed. But more as if he wants to savor this, savor me.

How can one person have such a wide range of kisses?

I melt into him, his hand still cradling my cheek. This kiss is so soft, so calm, completely opposite of the crazy rhythm beating in my chest. After just a moment, he pulls back.

Too short, the kiss leaves me wanting more.

But should I want more? Isn't this all too soon?

We pull apart, neither of us speaking as we watch the last of the night fade away to the colors of the day.

"Thank you for bringing me here," I say, nestled into the crook of his arm. "I won't ever forget this moment."

"You're welcome," Greg says. "It's one of my favorite places in the whole world. I've never shared it with anyone before. . . . I thought you'd enjoy it as much as I do."

"I do."

"You look a little chilly." Reaching to his side, Greg pulls a thermos off his waistband. "You up for some hot cocoa?"

"That sounds amazing."

Twisting off the cap, he fills it with the most amazing-smelling peppermint cocoa. I slide off my gloves and take the cap from him. Little wisps of steam rise from it, twisting and turning in the frozen air in front of me. I take a sip, and I'm immediately flooded by the sweet cocoa goodness as it warms me up from within.

"Is this your world-famous hot cocoa?" I ask him.

Greg nods, then smiles and looks at the ground.

"It's delicious. Just as good as the first time I tried it."

"Thanks," Greg says, adjusting in his seat. "Holly, I've been thinking." He looks up at me. "You remember how I said that all the unlucky things happening in your life, your relationship with Murphy, could be fate trying to get you back on track?"

I nod then take another sip of the cocoa.

"Well," says Greg after pausing to take a sip of cocoa from the thermos, "maybe it was fate that you came on this trip, that you were able to change so many things in your life and get it on a positive track."

"I'm not going to lie," I say, "I've been thinking about all that too. My life has changed completely since coming on this trip. And since I've broken up with Maverick and decided to start my own bakery, Murphy has seemed to be on my side. It feels like my life is back on course. It feels right." I touch my necklace, a proud reminder of how far I have come. "I'm looking forward to all the new possibilities and taking time to see what I want, what I need."

Greg nods, staying silent as I continue.

"I can't even tell you how grateful I am for you, Greg. Being my shoulder to cry on and helping me through the breakup with Maverick, encouraging me to follow my dreams, dreams I'd long since pushed aside and never thought I'd be able to go for. And then stepping up to help with the website and business side of things, that's just . . . wow." I'm feeling so blessed having Greg here with me. I truly couldn't have made it through the past couple of days without him. Reaching over, I set my hand on his forearm, and he lays his fingers on top of mine.

"Of course," says Greg, shrugging as if he hadn't played a huge part these past few days in the way my life has turned out.

"I'm really happy," I say, "that I came on this trip and that we could reconnect again. I'm not sure what happened to our friendship after high school, but I'm glad this vacation has helped us find it again."

"I am too," Greg says. "I've missed what we had growing up."

"Same," I say. I look at him, thinking about how easily we've stepped back into our friendship, like all those years apart were just a blip in time. It brings a smile to my face. "We had so many movie nights, video game marathons, camping adventures in the backyard under the stars, and ski trips. . . ."

"Remember that Sounds game in sixth grade?"

"How could I forget? I don't know what would've happened if you hadn't caught that ball," I say. "Thanks for always having my back, Greg." Moving my hand down to his, I squeeze it lightly.

I set my cap of cocoa next to me and then turn back to face Greg. Adjusting slightly in my seat, I prop my leg up between us so I can face him properly.

"Can I tell you something?" I ring my hands together, suddenly feeling nervous.

"Anything," Greg says without even a blink.

"I still have the baseball." I pause, then glance timidly at Greg. He's going to think I'm so weird keeping the ball after all this time. Who does that? Me. I do that. Why do I have such a hard time letting go of things? Surely Greg wouldn't know the baseball has meant so much to me.

He blinks, shaking his head. "I . . . uh, you do?"

"Yes, it sits on the bookshelf in my living room."

"Why do you still have it?" Greg asks, shocked. "After all these years. I thought you'd have gotten rid of it."

"Why would I get rid of it? It represents an important time from our childhood. A symbol of the four of us, friends forever, having fun and building memories together. I look at it and remember that day. It reminds me of you."

I think of the ball sitting on my shelf at home and how every time I saw it, Greg would instantly come to mind. I would remember the way he protected me from getting hit by the ball at the Sounds game and the worry in his eyes that I'd been hurt. I would remember the butterflies in my stomach when he'd held my hand to help me up and the sparks that burst through me when we hugged after he gave me the signed ball. And for some reason, I had wanted to hold on to those memories. Was it because I valued our friendship? Or was there another reason I'd held on to the ball all this time?

"I'm glad you've had something to remember me by," Greg says.

"Me too," I say. "But I have wondered, why did you give me the baseball?"

"It was yours," he replies, averting his eyes.

But I'm not buying that. He's the one that caught it. It was never mine. And what thirteen-year-old boy would just give away a signed baseball? There has to be another reason. "Greg, the real reason." I ask him again, "Why'd you give it to me?"

He blushes slightly, leans toward me a bit, and then admits, "Okay, honestly, I wanted you to have something to remind you that I would do anything for you, that I care about you, and that I'll always be there for you, Holly."

And he has always been there for me, not just this week in Snowden but growing up too. Remembering the Sounds game has me thinking about all the times he's been there for me in the past and again now.

"I'm so glad we've had this time together," Greg says. He looks over at me, his eyes filled with emotion. "And I don't think that this trip was only fated to rekindle our friendship. I think it was more than that. I think it was fate that brought the snowstorm after you arrived, that got me to come to the cabin earlier than I had originally planned, that delayed Gwen's and Trent's flights. All of that made it so that we could have alone time together . . . our first kiss."

I take a breath, trying to steady my erratic heart. I'm taken back to that moment in the kitchen. Our eyes locking in the darkened room. How I couldn't stop staring at him. Butterflies fluttering through me, and that kiss. Mmm . . . that kiss. Why is he saying this? Curious and a little nervous, my hand finds my necklace as I listen to him.

"We get along great together. We have amazing chemistry. We laugh and carry on like the years we've been apart haven't even happened. Our reconnecting this week came so easily. I feel like its fate pushing us to be together, to be more than just friends. I want to see if there is something. . . ." He trails off then looks at his feet and back to me. "Something between us."

Thoughts and emotions flood through me at rapid pace. They are so varied and come from so many places within me that I can't grasp on to any of them. I pull my eyes from Greg and look back out to the sunrise, trying to calm myself and take in what he just said.

I think of the past few days. I've really enjoyed spending them with Greg. Greg sees me. The real me, not the show I sometimes put on for others. But will it always feel this effortless? Could we last? Am I ready to try us out?

Greg is sweet, funny, and super hot. And he's right—our chemistry is indescribable. Our first kiss, it was everything. I've never been kissed like that. Could I start something with him? Should I risk our friendship and go all in? What if it turns out perfectly? But what if it ruins everything?

I just broke up with Maverick barely days ago. I know Maverick and Greg are so different, but I'm still finding myself. My emotions have been all over the place. Can I honestly rely on them now, no matter how good I feel about Greg? And what kind of woman breaks up with her boyfriend of three years, the man she thought she would marry, and then commits to a completely different man days later? What would that say about me? What would that say about my resolve to focus on myself?

And what about my bakery? I can't put my dreams on the backburner again. I need to focus on them and make sure they don't slip away. If I start another relationship, what would that mean for my dreams?

I know Greg would cherish me, be by my side no matter what, and that makes me feel so happy. But I've put my dreams on hold for too long. This is all happening too fast. I need time to process, to heal, to find me.

I clasp my hands together to steady them. "Greg, I'm thankful you brought me out here this morning. Sharing this beautiful spot and experience with me makes me feel so cherished."

I take a slow breath before looking back at Greg, his eyes so full of hope that it hurts me to continue. "This is a significant moment in my life. I'm finally feeling good about the direction it is taking, good about focusing on what I want." I reach up and grab the lotus necklace around my neck. "I bought this necklace to remind myself of that."

"It's beautiful," Greg says.

"Thanks. I bought it the other day when I was out shopping with Gwen. It's a lotus and a moonstone. The woman who sold it to me said they symbolize strength and overcoming difficulties. I felt drawn to it. It reminds me to have the confidence to focus on myself and be strong in the face of so much change. It makes me feel like I am enough and that I can do anything."

Greg nods. "It sounds like a perfect symbol for the change in your life."

I smile. "I think so too." Then I turn to Greg and take his hands in mine. He tilts his head at my embrace, curiosity flowing off him in waves. "Even though I know the change is good, it's overwhelming. I just broke up with Maverick, a man I spent too much time on and sacrificed much of my life for. I have so much emotional healing to do after ending things with him. On top of that, I'm changing careers. I'm starting a business. And from the past few days, I'm just beginning to understand how much work that will take. I'm so excited about it all. It's about time I focus on me and my dreams. But I also know it's going to take a lot of my time and energy."

I look into Greg's eyes, imploring him to understand as I continue, "Honestly, I'm a little scared that if I jump into another relationship, I will forget to focus on myself the way I need to. I'm afraid that my dreams will slip away again. I can't let that happen. I owe myself more than that."

Greg stays quiet, gently rubbing his thumb across my hand. He's entirely unreadable, and that makes me nervous. "I completely agree we have chemistry," I say. "I'd be a fool to deny that, and I do have feelings for you too. I don't want to give up on these feelings. I'm just conflicted, and I need time to process and think about everything."

He lets out a deep breath before turning his body to mirror mine. I'm silent. My chest hitches as my eyes grow teary.

Greg clears his throat. "I understand."

"I'm worried that this is all happening too fast . . . too soon. I need time to process these emotions before I can commit to a relationship. It wouldn't be fair to either of us."

My eyes are full of tears about to overflow. I don't want to ruin things with Greg. I really am feeling things for him, more than I've ever felt before. It's just so much. It's overwhelming.

Greg lightly brushes away a tear as it falls down my cheek.

Smiling softly, he cups the side of my face in his hand. "Holly, I know things just happened with your ex and that you are starting this new path for your life, so I understand that you need time to process everything. But I want you to know that I'm all in, and I'll wait for when you are ready for something too. I'm in no rush, all I ask is that you think about it. I can wait for you to be ready for us."

I let out a breath I didn't even know I was holding. Is Greg really okay with everything I just said? How is that possible? How is he not letting go of my hand, walking away, and leaving me here alone? His reaction is not what I expected.

Is it possible that I didn't ruin things by telling him how I feel? He's still here with me. He's holding my hand and smiling. How did I end up with a man like this sitting across from me?

I smile back as relief surges through me. "Thank you so much for understanding, Greg." I wrap my fingers more tightly around his as tears spring to my eyes.

"You're worth waiting for," he says.

CHAPTER 22
Greg

When we get back to the cabin, we notice a note on the back door. Holly reads it and, turning to me, she says, "Looks like Gwen and Trent went skiing. It'll just be us for a bit." I nod as she heads straight for the kitchen with a look of determination on her face. Barely taking time to remove her shoes, she's already across the cabin and pre-heating the oven.

My heart is still racing from our snowshoe outing. Holly kept the baseball. Never would I have thought she'd still have that baseball. That has to mean something, right? I'm disappointed she isn't ready to take a chance on a relationship with me. But I'm trying not to let myself get overwhelmed with grief. I get where she's coming from. It's just too soon, too much right now. I can reign in my feelings until she's ready. I have waited what feels like a lifetime already. What is a little longer? She is worth waiting for. If she doesn't want me, I will have to be okay with that too. I'll be the best supportive friend and let her know she deserves only the best. But I'm not going to lie to myself. I really want to be with her, more than I want my next breath.

Holly is focused on baking, and watching her concentrate, I'm just in awe of her. I stand there like a lovestruck fool, admiring Holly in her element. I feel a sense of relief now that I've talked to her. A calm that things will work out the way they are meant to. I will be the most patient man on the planet and let her lead whichever path we are meant to go down.

My heartbeat races, and I feel breathless as she pulls her sweater up over her head. The white tank top she's wearing underneath hugs her in all the right places, making my mouth go dry. She takes the "Enter at your own whisk" apron and throws it over her head then grabs a ton of items from the pantry and fridge.

Determination looks beautiful on her. There's something hot about her wearing something that I've worn. Yeah, I know it's just an apron, but damn. I could imagine her in one of my shirts and nothing else as she walks around with her bare legs, the sweet curves of her thighs peeking out.

"Kenton, are you okay?" Holly asks.

"Huh? Oh, yeah," I say, a little disappointed to be broken out of my fantasy.

"You have a glazed look on your face," she says. "What are you thinking about?"

I force an awkward laugh. "Just thinking about the website."

Yeah, like she's going to believe that. *Smooth cover, Greg.*

"Uh huh," she says, eyeing me skeptically. "Well, if you want to hang out in the kitchen, feel free. I'll just be cooking for the next few hours, so I'll be focused on that."

"No worries," I say, "I want to work on your website anyway."

Holly pulls out some measuring cups and a mixing bowl. "This place is going to smell so good in a few hours!" she says.

She sets a bag of coconut on the counter, and I'm instantly reminded of her vanilla-coconut scent. "It already smells wonderful," I say.

Oh, man. Get a grip. You've got a lot to do to get her website up and running. Stop daydreaming about Holly and get to work.

Shaking the thoughts of Holly out of my head, I head to the breakfast nook, making sure to sit far enough away to give her space for her baking, but not so far away that I can't admire her and remind her that I'm ready for us when she is.

Holly looks at home in the kitchen. Not even referencing a recipe, she measures out the ingredients. She's a vision, and there's a glow coming off her. It'd be clear to anyone that she is in paradise as she bakes.

After a few hours of working on the website and Holly finishing an assortment of baked goods, I walk into the kitchen. Examining her work, I say, "These look amazing."

"Thank you," she says, her cheeks growing pink as she adds some icing on top of a cake.

"Can I take a few pictures for the website?" I ask.

"Give me just a minute. I want them to look just right." She scurries around, adjusting the cookies, muffins, and cakes. Talking to herself under her breath, she adds little touches here and there. Finally, she gives me the go-ahead.

As I take pictures of the baked goods she's made, I can't help myself. I touch her every chance I can. Lightly holding her waist as I walk around her. Gently squeezing her hand as she admires the setup for each picture. Brushing her hair back when it falls in her face. Watching as a blush creeps up her cheeks, my own chest feeling so full.

"After these pictures are good to go," I say, "I'll need to get your domain set up."

"That's great," says Holly, smiling at me while she whips frosting in a bowl. "I'm so glad you know all the steps to setting up the website."

"That's what happens when you've done this a few dozen times," I say, taking a few pictures of some orange cinnamon muffins. "So what are you going to name it?"

"Name what?"

"The bakery," I say, turning my phone toward a peanut butter pie. "I'll need it for the domain name."

"Right," says Holly, "I haven't thought about that yet." She takes a spoon and dips it in the frosting before lifting it to her mouth and tasting it. "Don't get me wrong," she continues, "everything about this path feels right. There's just so much to figure out."

"Yep, starting a business is not for the faint of heart," I say, adjusting my camera for another picture.

"What do you think about a name?" she asks.

I look at her incredulously. "You want my advice on naming your bakery?"

"Yes," she says, smiling. "I trust you."

My heart beats rapidly at her statement. She trusts me. That's huge. Right? After everything she's gone through, I feel honored that she feels this way about me. A warm feeling spreads through me. Hope.

"Okay, what about Chessie Valley Bakery?"

"No, too generic," she says.

"Baked Goods by Holly?"

She shakes her head. Then she bounces up and down excitedly. "We should do something like one of the sayings on your mom's aprons. Something fun and quirky that would bring a smile to people's faces."

I give a little chuckle at the thought, "Always trying to make others happy, that sounds just like a Holly thing to do."

She blushes.

"Okay, let's think," I say. "Bake Me Happy?"

She wrinkles her nose.

"Okay, no." I give another idea. "What about All You Knead, but knead like dough?"

"No, that doesn't make sense," she says before biting her bottom lip.

"What about something with your name? Holly and Icing?" I ask.

"No, doesn't have the ring to it, the feeling that I want." Her eyes sparkle with anticipation. Gears must be turning in her head.

"Hmm . . . okay, this is tricky."

"Right?" she says.

I nod, standing up and pacing back and forth. "Cakes, Muffins, Sugar . . ." I murmur to myself. "What about For the Love of Sugar?" I suggest, raising my eyebrows as I wait for her response.

Clasping her hands to her chest, Holly's eyes shoot up to me. "Oh. My. Gosh. It's perfect!" She squeals, jumping up and down before running over to wrap her arms around me. I still for a moment then relax into her embrace, wrapping my arms around her. I lay my head against hers enjoying this moment however brief. I feel so blessed that she let me be a part of such a huge piece of her new life.

After a couple more hours of baking and working on the website, Holly plops down at the breakfast nook with me. She rests her head on the back of the bench and closes her eyes. She's baked herself to the bone. Her apron is covered in chocolate and peanut butter, her cheek has a smudge of flour on it, and her hair is coming out of her ponytail. It only adds to her beauty.

Before I can stop myself, I reach out and tuck a strand of her chestnut hair behind her ear. Her eyes snap open then lock with mine.

"Sorry, you have a loose strand," I say sheepishly. "And you have a little flour just there." I point to her cheek.

She wipes near where I pointed, not quite getting it.

"Here, let me," I say. She stills, and I reach over and hold her face in my palm. She leans into my hand, and I brush the flour away with my thumb. Her eyes look into mine, and we take each other in. A spark that could set the house on fire lights within me.

She leans closer to me, and I want more.

So much more.

But I can't act on it. I can't act on the fire burning inside me. I can't pull her close, gather her in my arms, and kiss her. I can't put my physical needs before her emotional ones. She needs time to process, to decide if she wants me, if she wants us.

She's my person, my forever. She always has been and always will be.

No one has ever or could ever compare to her.

If things don't work out between us, there'll never be another girl that makes me feel the way she does. This has to work out.

It has to.

My very heart—my soul—depends on it. I can't jeopardize our future by doing something impulsive now.

I slowly drop my palm from her face.

Holly's brow furrows in confusion.

Not sure how to explain why I don't want to kiss her right now and hoping to still show her that I want her, I simply take her hand in mine.

"Do you want to see what I've done so far?" I ask, nodding toward my laptop.

Holly blinks. "Um, yeah," she says, her brow still furrowed.

I smile, and with my free hand, I slide the laptop in front of us.

When I pull up her webpage, her eyes go wide. "Wow, this is beautiful!" she says. "You're really talented."

"Thanks," I say, my face going a bit red. "I haven't been able to do work like this in a while, and it's fun for me."

We spend the next few minutes discussing fonts and image layout. "Okay," I say, "it looks like we're ready to add in those pictures."

"Are you sure?" she asks.

"Absolutely. Here, hand me my phone, and I'll get them uploaded."

Holly picks up my phone but keeps it in her hand. "Do you think what I baked looks good enough to go on a website?" she asks and then chews on her lip.

"They look and smell amazing," I tell her sincerely.

She swats my arm, laughing. "You can't smell a picture."

"Well the food smells amazing, and the pictures look like you can reach in, take them out, and eat them."

"I'd say that it's a success then," she says, handing me my phone.

Our hands briefly touch, and I pause, smiling at her. *Good grief, Greg, get a grip. Let's get the website finished,* I think.

I take the phone from her hand and turn back to my laptop to download the pictures.

"Do you know what you're calling the baked goods you'll be selling?" I ask her. "I can add little captions for each image."

Holly stands and paces around the breakfast nook. "So, umm, there's the obvious, more traditional Snickerdoodle

Macarons and Hummingbird Cake," she says slowly before biting her lip again.

Why does she seem nervous to tell me the names she's come up with? They can't be that bad, right?

Tilting my head slightly, I look at her with raised eyebrows.

A nervous giggle escapes her. Then she pauses her pacing, squares her shoulders, and says, "Sunrise Sin for the orange cinnamon muffins, Chocolate Ecstasy for the chocolate cupcakes, On Cloud Nine for the lemon meringue pie, Cobble Me Up for the boysenberry cobbler, Whip It Good for the whipped peanut butter pie, and Butter Me Up Bars for the coconut bars." She finishes in a rush, her face growing from pink to beet red in mere seconds.

I'm still as a statue. The names she's come up with remind me of all the things I want to do to her. I run my hands through my hair, trying to calm the heat that's rushing through me.

"You don't like the names, do you?" she whispers, rocking back and forth from heel to toe.

"Like them?" I say, a slow grin spreading across my face. "I love them. I think they're clever and fun. They'll give character to your products."

"You think so?"

"You're brilliant," I say, locking my eyes with hers.

She beams, and I'm breathless as my heart leaps at the joy on her face.

"I'll get going on adding those names to the website," I say. "And after that, I'm thinking of order forms, meetings for quotes, pages devoted to the different things you make, and prices, of course. You can have specials for the week and stuff like that. If there's anything you don't like, we can change it. This is your future, your career. It should be exactly how you want it to be."

Suddenly Holly wraps me in a hug. I'm so caught off guard that it takes me a minute before I wrap my arms around her in return.

"You're amazing," she says.

"I'd do anything for you," I tell her.

"Thank you, Greg," she says. "You have no idea how much this means to me. After the past few years, I never thought I'd be looking forward to what my future holds."

"You deserve everything you've ever wanted Holly," I say, wrapping my arms more tightly around her.

CHAPTER 23
Holly

I can't believe how much we've gotten done today. Greg truly is amazing. My website is colorful and whimsical, exactly what I never knew I wanted. It looks professional. Well, I guess it is since Greg is a professional, but somehow, he makes me look like I'm a professional baker. I don't know where my future would be without all his hard work today.

Working alongside Greg was effortless. Everything seems so easy. Is this what life would be like with him? Full of fun and laughter, simple, not complicated?

The more time I spend with him, the more I want to be around him. He makes me feel validated, like what I have to say matters. Am I ready to take on another relationship? One with Greg would be serious, not just a fling. And he is totally correct. We have great chemistry together. I know he would never hurt me, so what is causing me to not take the leap?

Am I scared? Maybe a little. Though I don't think it's because I fear a relationship with him. I fear reverting back to what I was with Maverick.

I smile at Greg, who's sitting next to me on the couch in the movie room. After a day of hard work, we decided to take a break and watch a movie.

"What do you want to watch?" asks Greg, taking a bite of one of my snickerdoodle macarons.

I scroll through the streaming service before spotting *Jumanji: Welcome to the Jungle.* "What about this one?" I ask. "It's funny."

"I'll take your word for it. I haven't seen it before."

"What! Who are you? Do you live in a cave or something? How have you not seen it before?"

Greg chuckles at my outburst. "I don't do much for fun, remember?"

"Well, when you move home, we can remedy that." I laugh, pushing play on the movie.

"Oh, really, what'd you have in mind?" he asks, giving me a playful grin.

"You are hilarious," I say, smacking him on the arm. "You know what I meant."

I hear my words replay in my head. *When you move home, we can remedy that.* I mean it though, whether we end up in a relationship or not. I treasure our friendship. I would want to spend time with him. Whether he is just a friend or my boyfriend.

I think about what Greg said when we were watching the sunrise. How he wants to be with me. Is there a future for us? We've been stuck at this cabin together. Two people brought together by a freak storm. Was that Murphy possibly working his magic to put me back on my correct path?

Greg and I together does feel right though, doesn't it? Would I even know? Can I trust my own judgment? I haven't had a good sense of what's best for me in quite a while apparently. I grasp my necklace in my hand, lightly tracing the outline of the lotus. If such a beautiful flower can push past and overcome, then surely I can too. I can learn to trust my instincts.

I've never felt as cared for and safe as I've felt with Greg. He's shown me so much kindness. Not to mention his kisses make me feel things. Feelings that have no right being stirred inside me. A hope I shouldn't be feeling. Or should I? Greg laid everything out to me. He is giving me the chance to decide what I want to do, what I want us to be.

As the movie starts, I get sucked in.

I gasp and laugh along with the movie. Every now and then Greg chuckles too.

Greg grabs a coconut bar off our plate piled with a mountain of desserts. I smile at him, and he returns it with an adorable half grin.

When the four actors are in a market and one eats some cake, I giggle to myself, knowing what's coming next. Greg eyes me curiously, but I don't say a thing.

Suddenly the actor who had eaten the cake explodes.

Greg looks aghast.

My stomach hurts from trying to hold in my silent giggles.

"I'll *never* look at a piece of cake the same way," Greg says.

Unable to help myself, I laugh aloud, letting out a snort, which makes me laugh even harder.

"Not funny," Greg says. "Cake is my favorite!"

"I just can't with your face right now," I say, laughing through the tears.

"That's it," Greg says, standing, a playful smile on his face. "I can't watch this movie if it's going to ruin any other desserts for me."

"Wait!" I exclaim, grabbing his arm. "You can't begin a movie and not finish it . . . especially if you haven't seen it before."

I draw him back toward the couch. I pull a little harder than I'd intended, and Greg topples on top of me.

"Oh my gosh. I'm so sorry," I say, heat flushing my face. With his body pressed against mine, my heart beats erratically.

Greg's eyes turn from playful to fiery in less than a breath.

As we stare into each other's eyes, I want to stay like this forever. The seconds tick by as I take him in. I feel every line of his abs against my stomach, see every divot that forms his muscular arms. Five seconds have passed.

His lips look soft, and the stubble on his chin is so masculine that I lean toward him. Six seconds.

His smoky cinnamon scent is intoxicating, and I need his lips against mine. Seven seconds.

Gulping, I try to calm my ever-increasing heart rate as I lean closer and closer toward him. I'm one hundred percent sure I'm about to go into cardiac arrest at the way my heart is pounding. Eight seconds.

Our lips are a whisper away, and I'm anticipating a kiss that will spread sparks through my limbs and a heat that will wholly envelop me. Nine seconds.

But then Greg distances his mouth from mine and presses his lips against my forehead.

Wait, what? The fire that was building within me quickly diminishes as he pulls away from me. Did I read everything wrong? Had we not stared into each other's eyes an inordinate amount of time?

Greg sits up on the couch. Smiling, he asks, "So are we going to finish this movie or what?"

Unable to comprehend what didn't just happen, I only nod as I gather myself and turn to the screen.

We watch the movie in silence, the occasional chuckle coming from Greg.

But I can't focus on the movie. All I can think about is what happened between Greg and me. Why did he kiss my forehead? That was the last thing I expected. Couldn't he feel what I was feeling? Didn't he want me as much as I wanted him in that moment? What happened to that fiery look that he had?

Now that I think about it, he didn't kiss me at the breakfast nook earlier either. I mean, I thought I was clearly giving all the signals to kiss me then and now. I could have sworn my thoughts were so loud all of Snowden could hear them.

Is he having second thoughts? Does he not want to be with me anymore? What the heck is going on? I pause my downward thoughts. *Okay, Holly, no freaking out.*

The movie ends, and Greg gets up, taking my empty plate from me.

"That was a good movie," he says as we enter the kitchen, "though it still ruined cake for me." He eyes the remainder of the cake sitting on the kitchen counter and gives me a half grin.

I nod, returning a half-hearted smile.

We clean up our plates, putting away the rest of the baked goods I'd made earlier. I really did go a bit overboard. When we finish, we walk upstairs in silence.

Reaching my bedroom door, I'm just about to turn my doorknob when Greg says, "Holly, I . . ." but then he trails off.

I open my door, about to take a step inside, when Greg reaches out to stop me. "Holly, wait."

He runs a hand through his dark brown hair, messing it up even more than it already is. Why'd he have to do that? I want to reach up and run my fingers through his hair.

"You okay, Kenton?" I ask.

"I don't want to make things weird," he says, "and I don't know how to . . ."

He reaches out to take my hand, brushing his lips softly against the tops of my fingers.

I gaze at him, his eyes studying me. I'm so confused. I know he has something on the tip of his tongue. Why can't he just say it? Is it because he changed his mind? Does he not think we would be good together anymore? That we couldn't be happy?

"Holly, I . . ."

My heart races at his tone. I look down at our hands as he intertwines his fingers with mine. My eyes widen, emotion sparking within. I look up at Greg as he wraps his other arm around my waist and pulls me in close to him. I lean against him, and my heart beats fast against my chest.

Unlinking his right hand from mine, he gently caresses my face. His hand feels rough against my soft skin, his thumb sweeping across my cheek. Back and forth, back and forth. I'm lost in his eyes, the heat of his body. I want to be close to him. Our bodies are so close and yet so far. Without thinking about what I'm doing, I grab his sweater. Gently, I pull it over his head. As it drops to the ground, I run my hands over his chest.

His eyes flash with desire. "Holly," he whispers. His hands trail down the side of my body, reaching the bottom of my top. He slowly inches the shirt up, stopping just below my bra.

"Are we moving too . . . Is this okay?" he asks.

Yes! This is more than okay. Say it. Tell him. To heck with all my half-baked doubts. Not having him with me feels wrong. Physically, emotionally, all of it. No matter what my insecurities say. But the words won't come. They get caught in my throat.

Unable to speak, I just nod. The fact that he stopped to ask, to check on me, it opens my heart. Actions speak louder than words anyway, right? I lift my top over my head and drop it on the floor. His hands move over my bare skin. Our bodies shiver in anticipation.

Tilting my head up slightly toward him, my gaze flicks from his eyes to his lips to his bare chest and back to his eyes. He presses his lips gently against mine. I feel his tenderness and how he's holding back.

A soft moan of longing breaks through me, telling him everything he needs to know. He presses his lips harder against me, deepening the kissing and pulling my body flush to his. My arms wrap around his neck, pulling him in closer. I want him. I need him. My whole body reacts to his, my legs wobbly at the emotions flowing through me.

Heat flares within me, scorching me at the close contact and causing every nerve ending to be on high alert. My body reacts to his like it never has to another. Greg lets go of my waist only to run his hand up my back, guiding us both toward the wall.

The cold of the wall is a stark contrast to the warmth of our bodies. I slide a hand into his hair at the base of his neck, and he moans into my mouth. Our tongues exploring, tasting, devouring each other. I can't get enough of him. Our hands run over each other's bodies. Our mouths try desperately to be as close to each other as we can, barely leaving room for heated breaths. My heart races as thoughts ricochet around in my head.

How far am I willing to go? Part of me wants to be all in. But I'm not a one-night-stand kind of girl. Can we go further without strings attached? Is that fair to Greg?

What would be the consequences? Do I care? Yes, of course I care. I don't want to hurt him. I care for him. He makes me feel special. Cared for. Beautiful. I am all in on this. I want him, and the way he is cradling me, running his hands over my skin and pulling me against him, makes me know he wants me too.

"Greg," I say, moaning as he leaves a trail of kisses down my neck.

"Yeah?" he asks, not stopping.

"Do you want to . . ." I suck in a breath as he nibbles on my earlobe, the sensation causing shivers to jolt through me.

"Do you want to head in there?" I ask, motioning to my room.

A wide smile breaks across his face. He opens his mouth to speak but is cut off from a noise downstairs.

But we don't break body contact. Instead, he places his forehead against mine, both of us breathless. His hands still rest on my waist.

A moment goes by, and we hear Gwen and Trent talking downstairs.

"You've got to be kidding me," Greg says.

"Good thing they came in now," I whisper. "It would have been really awkward if they'd walked in on us, considering they have no clue about, well, about us."

"If you think they don't know about us," Greg says, "then you've lost your mind."

My stomach clenches. What did he just say?

Suddenly all I see is Maverick in front of me. Maverick telling me I've lost my mind at the slopes. Maverick berating me, putting me down. Maverick holding me back from my dreams. Maverick cheating on me. Maverick pinning me against this wall.

Panic spreads through me. I feel sick. I want his hands off me. I don't want them on my waist or my neck. I don't want his body pressed against mine. My pulse races, and my ears ring.

I'm frantic. I need space. I need to get away.

I see a blur of Greg and Maverick. They're just the same, playing games with me for their own personal gain. Greg has been holding back just to toy with me, to increase my want for him. Just so he can have his way. Then what? We have sex, and I become yesterday's news?

I struggle against him. This was just some same-time-same-place kind of fling. He doesn't really have feelings for me. He was just saying that, just like Maverick. If I stay with him, I'll be right back where I was. It'll be the same situation, different name. I'd be swapping one Maverick for another. And I can't let this ruin everything. I can't let that happen.

My necklace burns against my chest. I'm picking me. I'm picking my dreams and my goals. I'm not going to let another man stop me from doing that.

Pushing him away, I look desperately for my shirt.

Finding it, I throw it back on just as I hear Gwen and Trent coming up the stairs.

"Holly?" Greg asks. "What's wrong?" He looks panicked and confused standing shirtless in the hallway.

I turn into my room, trying to stop the tears from trailing down my cheeks.

"Holly, wait," Greg says.

"I can't do this."

"What?" Greg asks. "Can't do what?"

"Us," I say, closing my bedroom door.

CHAPTER 24
Greg

The click of the lock as Holly closes her bedroom door is deafening.

"Holly!" I say, both my hands on her door. I'm desperate. What happened? Why is she so upset? What went so wrong? We were fine. We were more than fine. I run a hand through my hair. I don't get it. She wanted us. She wanted me. She's the one who started all of this, the one who wanted to take it further. . . . And then she was just gone.

My stomach drops. Sick. I feel sick. I've ruined everything, and I don't even know what I've done wrong.

I turn my head to see Gwen and Trent at the top of the stairs.

"Dude, what happened?" asks Trent. "You don't look so good."

"Where's Holly?" asks Gwen, flicking her eyes at my shirtless top.

I look at them, but I have no words. I can't answer their questions. I don't know what just happened. I need to think. I need to get away from this hallway.

I grab my sweater and pull it over my head, heading downstairs.

At the bottom of the stairs, I glance back. Gwen and Trent haven't moved. They both have expressions on their faces that I can't deal with right now. Holly's door is still shut. I nod curtly, my soul crumbling as I turn away from the woman who has my whole heart.

Tears prick at the back of my eyes. My heart feels like it's shattered into a million pieces. I messed things up. I went too far and lost my chance.

I stride down the stairs, through the den, and onto the deck before collapsing onto one of the rocking chairs. I lean my head on my hands, silent tears flowing. What happened? I replay the scene over and over, but I can't figure out what went wrong.

I asked her if we needed to slow down. I would have stopped for her. I'd told her I would wait for her to be ready, and I'd meant it. But she gave me the go-ahead. Didn't she? Did I read that all wrong?

The frantic look on her face as she pushed me away, her big emerald eyes shining with unshed tears. It cut to my core. I've messed up. Ruined everything.

The door to the porch creaks open. I don't look up.

"Dude, it's cold out here," says Trent, pulling up a chair next to me, "and you don't have a jacket."

"I'm not cold," I manage to say as Gwen sits down next to me too.

"Greg," Gwen says, her voice tight and stern. "What just happened up there?"

I don't say anything.

"Holly wouldn't open her door," Gwen continues. "She wouldn't even respond when I knocked."

"Talk to us," Trent says. "We've got your back."

I don't want to talk about this. I don't want to talk to them about messing things up with Holly.

But I don't know what went wrong, and I don't know what to do. I need them to help me make sense of all this.

"I've ruined everything," I say.

"I seriously doubt that, dude," says Trent. "She's crazy for you."

A painful tightness clutches at my throat, but I manage to respond. "Maybe she was but not anymore. I went too far."

Gwen stiffens, but doesn't say anything.

"And now I've lost her," I continue.

"Greg," says Gwen sternly, "tell us what happened."

"Maybe it was all a misunderstanding?" adds Trent.

"I seriously doubt that," I say.

"Tell us," Gwen says again.

I tilt my head back in my seat and tell them everything we'd done that day: snowshoeing, working on the website, and baking. I briefly touch on the almost kisses in the kitchen. They hear about the movie and then that we kissed in the hallway, stopping after we heard them come in. Finally, I tell them how hurt Holly looked and how she had wanted to get away from me as quickly as possible. When I finish, they're completely silent.

"Will one of you say something?" I yell, as fear envelopes me. Have I really lost Holly?

"It, it doesn't make sense," says Gwen. "Nothing that you've told us should have caused her to react that way."

"Did you tell us everything?" Trent prompts.

"Yes, I did," I say, dropping my head back into my hands.

"Why would she physically and emotionally push you away like that?" asks Gwen.

"I don't know," I say.

I breathe in a ragged breath. "I just wish I understood what'd I'd done so I can fix it."

"I'll go talk to her," says Gwen.

"No, let me," says Trent, standing. "I haven't gotten a chance to talk to Holly in a while anyway."

Gwen nods.

"Greg, don't give up," Trent says. "I'm sure there's a reason behind all of this."

I hope he's right. I'm devastated. I don't know what I'll do if Holly's not in my life. I could never forgive myself if I'd hurt her in some way.

CHAPTER 25
Holly

A light knock at my door breaks me out of my daze. Gwen had knocked on the door earlier, but I had turned her away. I didn't want her to get mixed up in all this. Wasn't this exactly what she had been worried about? That trying things out with her brother would get messy, and she'd be stuck in the middle of it? Shortly after Gwen stopped knocking on my door, Margot called, but I sent her to voicemail. I couldn't face either of them right then.

"I'm fine, G," I say, but my teary voice doesn't even convince myself.

"It's not Gwen. It's Trent."

Trent? I thought he'd be downstairs with Greg.

"Would you let me in, please?" Trent asks.

I slowly manage to get up from the loveseat and open the door just a crack.

"Hi," I say, wiping a tear from my cheek.

"Hi, can I come in?" asks Trent. "I was hoping to talk to you."

It's not often that I see Trent with a solemn face. "Sure," I say and open the door wider, motioning for him to come in.

I know I must look a mess because all I've been doing since I left Greg in the hallway is sitting on this loveseat bawling my eyes out.

"Thanks," he says, walking over to the little loveseat and sitting down. I give a small smile seeing his long frame folded awkwardly on top of it.

I lower myself next to him, crossing my legs and turning toward him.

"Are you okay?" he asks.

"No," I say then burst into tears. He pulls me into him, wrapping me in a hug.

After my crying settles and my breath steadies, Trent says, "I know you probably don't want to talk about it."

I shake my head.

"And you don't have to," Trent continues. "I don't need or want to know what happened between you and Greg. I just want to tell you something."

I nod, letting him know I'm listening.

"Greg has liked you for thirteen years now."

My head snaps up at this confession.

"What?" I say, completely taken aback. Thirteen years? That would mean that Greg had feelings for me before this trip. "Yes, you heard me right," Trent says. "Greg has liked you for over a decade. He has always kept his distance from you because he didn't know how to act on his feelings, first as a kid and then as a teen and adult. But these past few days, that's changed. He's been trying to find the courage to tell you that he likes you. And I think that has a lot to do with him feeling comfortable with you, and maybe even you feeling a similar way toward him."

My eyes fill with tears again. "I can't be with someone who is going to hurt me, belittle me, think less of me. Not again."

"I know," says Trent. "Maverick was horrible, and I never want you to be with someone like that again."

I wipe a tear from my eye.

"But, Holly," Trent continues, "you've got to know that Greg would never hurt you, not intentionally anyway. He's a good guy. One of the best. Right now, he is downstairs shattered at the thought that he hurt you. I'm sure whatever happened, Greg didn't mean anything bad by it. I promise you, Holly, I have never seen him so all in on anyone in my entire life. He would rather die a thousand deaths than ever hurt you."

A thought runs through my head, one of the thoughts from the hallway: *This was just some same-time-same-place kind of fling. He doesn't really have feelings for me. He was just saying that, just like Maverick.* But if what Trent says is true, Greg has had feelings for me for thirteen years, meaning everything this weekend was years in the making. That would be a really long time for someone to wait just to play games with my heart. That must mean that everything he's been saying and doing has been genuine. My breath hitches at the realization. He couldn't be like Maverick at all then, could he?

"I say all this to you," says Trent, "not to tell you what to do or how to feel. You've had someone do that to you for way too long, and it's time you take control of your life. But I hope you find it within you to see Greg for who he truly is and to not confuse him and his goodness for what you fear might happen again."

I nod my head yet again, unsure what to say at this point. I am wholly unsure of what I feel anymore.

With that, Trent leans over and tucks me into a big bear hug, the kind only big brothers can give. "Oh, and Holly," he says, standing, "we're going skiing tomorrow. I know you haven't wanted to since the last time you went the whole Maverick thing happened, but you need to overcome that. And with the four of us together, nothing can stop the fun that's sure to ensue."

I can't help but crack a smile at that.

He leaves me to think, whispering, "Night, Holly," before he closes my bedroom door.

I sit there a bit longer, recapping everything Trent said. After a few minutes, I feel exhausted emotionally and physically. I lie down in bed, hoping to get some sleep. I curl the blankets up around my neck and hold onto the pillow.

But sleep doesn't come. I toss and turn for what feels like forever. Finally I look up at the ceiling and let more thoughts and emotions flood through me.

Am I ready to go skiing again? Am I ready to spend more time with Greg? I am definitely attracted to him, and it's clear that he is attracted to me. We'd be fools to think otherwise, but there's more to it than that. I feel different with him than I'd felt with Maverick. I feel cared for.

I think of the baseball he gave me so many years ago. Of course I kept it to remember our friendship, but it was something else too. There was something else from that day that I wanted to remember, but I can't quite make out what it was.

Greg is so attentive to my needs. Being there for me on the slopes the day Maverick showed up and calming my anger and sadness in the kitchen. Seeing me for me and noticing that I wasn't happy with my job. Offering up his vacation time to help me create a website from scratch for a brand-new business. The thoughts and reasons go on and on.

Trent is right. Greg is a good guy. I know that. I know he doesn't want to hurt me. It wasn't him that caused me to panic. It was what he said. Those words "you've lost your mind" triggered me. And I am only now realizing just how deeply Maverick wounded me. I need Greg to understand how deeply Maverick hurt me and how much healing I have to do.

Maybe this will all be too much for Greg. For me. Maybe I'm not ready to try something with Greg. But I can't deny how drawn I am to him and how safe he makes me feel. Is there some way we could make this work? Is there some way Greg could understand that I want to move forward with us but at the same time am terrified to move forward with us?

My head spins, and I can't settle down. Maybe some warm milk and cinnamon will put me at ease so I can finally sleep.

CHAPTER 26
Greg

It's late, but I can't sleep. I sit in front of the fireplace, my stomach in knots. I can't stop thinking about what happened with Holly. Where did it go wrong? Was it something I said? Was it something I did?

Why did I have to mess things up? We could've been happy.

But now I'll never know, will I? Why? Because I let my physical needs blind me from my decision to allow her to take time to heal, to figure things out. Is it too late for us? Did I mess up so bad that we can't come back from this?

I hear someone coming down the stairs. I glance at my watch. It's 2:00 a.m. Why would anyone be up this late?

Then I see my favorite messy bun, one that belongs to the woman who holds my heart, Holly. At the sight of her, my breath leaves my body and my stomach clenches. Could I ever get her back?

"Holly?" I whisper.

"Oh!" She gasps, jumping at the sound of my voice. "I didn't know anyone else was up. I couldn't sleep."

"Me either," I say.

I watch her intently, searching her face. She studies me, like she's trying to peer into my soul. I want so badly to hold her, to kiss away her worries. To make everything better. One thing I'm sure of is that before I messed up, she'd felt safe and cared for when I'd hold her. I wish we could go back to that.

"Why can't you sleep?" Holly asks.

"I couldn't sleep after . . ." I trail off, terrified I'm going to do or say something to make her run again. "Holly, I—"

"Greg, I'm—" she says at the same time.

I give her a half-hearted smile, nodding for her to continue.

She lowers her gaze, twirling a loose strand of her hair. "I feel like, well . . . I owe you an apology."

"What?" I shake my head. Why does she want to apologize? "No. Holly, you don't owe me an apology."

I stand up and step toward her, then I hesitate, not sure that she wants me near her.

She looks up and locks her eyes with mine. She seems nervous, but then she takes a small step toward me.

And that's the only sign I need. I walk toward her, and we meet in the middle of the living room, inches apart from each other.

She takes a deep, pained breath. Her eyes close. "Yes, yes I do. You didn't deserve how I reacted. It's just that something you said reminded me of how Maverick used to treat me, and all of the emotions I had with Maverick came rushing back. I wasn't thinking right. I unfairly put all of those feelings on you."

"What?" I say, completely shocked. The last thing I want is to remind Holly of Maverick. I swallow and say, "I'm so sorry. I don't even know what to say. I never want to treat you the way Maverick did or make you feel the way he did."

"It's not your fault. You couldn't have known."

"Well, I don't want to mess up like that again. What was it that I said that reminded you . . ." The knots in my stomach tighten. ". . . of him?"

"When you were talking about Gwen and Trent knowing about us, you said 'You've lost your mind.'"

The instant she says those words, I'm brought back to that moment on the slopes. I heard Maverick say that exact phrase to her when he was ending things, or pretending to end things. My stomach drops.

"Plus," Holly continues, "with you pulling back earlier in the day in the kitchen and on the couch during the movie, I just thought in the moment that you were playing games with me like Maverick did. I know it's stupid, but it's just that he always talked down to me and played with my emotions, and it triggered me."

Her eyes fill with tears, and I can't help but take her hands in mine, closing the distance between us. I rub her hands between mine, staying quiet as she continues.

"I just need you to be patient with me. I'm still healing. I realized tonight how deeply Maverick scarred me. So much has happened this week, and it's all so overwhelming. My emotions are all over the place, and you don't deserve that."

I let go of one of her hands to tilt her head up so I can look into her stunning green eyes. "I'm sorry I wasn't as sensitive to your needs as I should have been. You have every right to feel every emotion you are feeling. You've been hurt so long, it's not something you can get over in a night. But Holly, I will never—" My voice catches. "I could never live with myself if I treated you the way Maverick did. I want you to know that I pulled back because I promised you that I would be patient. That I would wait for you to be ready for something between us. I just didn't want to rush you physically or emotionally. I want you, Holly. I've always wanted you. I never meant for you to feel unwanted. Any time you're ready to take another step—I'll be there."

"I know," she says, touching my cheek.

I still at her touch, not daring to pull away or lean into it. My body frozen, barely a breath leaves me.

"You're nothing like Maverick," she says, looking into my eyes. "I know you would never hurt me. I know you just want to support me. You stood up for me countless times when you didn't have to. You make me feel like I can do anything, be anything. You've taken your well-earned time off to build me a whole website for my bakery. You understood me when we watched the sunrise and I explained I needed more time to figure things out. And . . ." Her voice cracks with emotion. "And you have been protecting me since we were kids, not letting that darn baseball hit me." Her eyes gleam with fresh tears.

I reach up to gently brush away her tears as they lightly fall down her soft cheek. "I will always look out for you. But not because I have to, because I want to. And I will be more careful, more considerate of your past and your emotions."

"And I will communicate better and try not to freak out when I feel triggered. Instead I promise to tell you so you are aware."

"I can be as patient as you need for however long you need."

"Thank you, Greg," she says. "You're amazing."

I lightly squeeze her hand. Holly wraps her fingers around mine and says, "I would like to try . . . try to see what we can be together."

My head snaps up. What did she just say?

"But I need to go slowly," Holly continues. "Like maybe snail pace. And you have to know that there will be times when my past gets triggered, but I will be open and honest with you about everything."

Is she giving me another chance? Does she want to try us out? My heart is so full of emotion I feel like I can't breathe from the intensity of it. In and out, slow and steady.

Holly inches closer to me. The yearning in her eyes causes a hyperawareness inside me that pierces my heart and makes it jolt. She raises up on her toes and kisses me oh so softly. Her lips are perfect, sweet, and soft against mine. Though it's only been a few hours, it feels like a lifetime ago since our lips last touched.

The soft kiss doesn't turn into anything more. It doesn't have to. It's absolute perfection. She knows I care for her. She knows I wouldn't hurt her. She knows I would do anything for her. And that's all I need.

I kiss her softly on the forehead. Though I want everything with her, I can and will be patient. I will be the man she needs me to be.

"Thank you for understanding," Holly says softly.

I nod and pull her into me, enveloping her in my arms.

"Can we just sit together for a bit?" Holly asks.

I nod, leading her to the couch. We sit, our hands intertwined. Holly wraps her free hand around my arm and leans next to me. I brush back a strand of hair that has fallen across her face, grazing her soft cheek with my hand. She looks up to me with her big, round eyes, and I kiss the top of her forehead again.

Maybe everything will be okay. It's almost impossible to maintain a chill exterior as internally, my emotions are going off like fireworks on the Fourth of July.

She wants to be with me.

When I thought just moments ago that all was lost, relief has surged in despair's place. A renewed sense that I can be the man for Holly. We may hit some roadblocks along the way, but we have a plan to tackle those together.

Together.

That word fills me with more joy than I could imagine. Leaning my head against hers, I sit in companionable silence with her. I feel the rise and fall of her chest against my arm. Just being next to her and listening to the sound of her soft breathing calms my fears of losing her. I slowly lean back into the couch and close my eyes.

CHAPTER 27
Holly

My eyes flutter open as light streams in through the window. Greg is sleeping soundly next to me on the couch. I guess we fell asleep here last night.

A few days ago, I would have panicked seeing him next to me, but right now, it's perfect. I'm at peace. I feel a change happening inside me. Pieces clicking into place. I'm not the same woman I was when I first got to Snowden. So much has changed.

Greg slowly stirs. Just seeing him beside me fills me with happiness. He's nothing like Maverick, just as Trent said. I don't know why I ever questioned him.

I don't know if I'll ever be bold enough to tell Greg that he's shattered the wall around my heart, unable to be rebuilt. But it gives me hope. Hope that I'm finally on the right path and that one day I could tell him.

I sit up. Excitement for the day floods through me. Though I'm hesitant to go back to where Maverick initially broke up with me, I'm excited that all four of us will be together today.

You're on my side today, Murphy . . . right? No crazy mishaps? No looking like a fool in front of Greg?

I take the silence as confirmation, deciding Murphy and I are on the same team now. Best friends if you will.

"Morning," Greg says, grabbing my hand. He gives it a light kiss as he stirs awake.

"Morning," I say. I can't help but smile at him.

He pushes a strand of hair back from my forehead. "Looks like we fell asleep."

"Looks like it," I say.

He kisses me softly on the forehead, and I snuggle back into him.

"Well, what do we have here?" says Trent, coming down the stairs. He's grinning from ear to ear.

I feel my ears turning red.

Gwen is right behind Trent but looking much groggier than he does.

She heads into the kitchen, and we follow her.

Greg hands me a bowl. I smile and gently bite my lip.

"What are you smiling about?" Gwen says in a monotone voice, pouring herself some coffee. "Is it because of what I saw on the couch this morning?"

I blush again. How could I have thought that Gwen and Trent had no idea about Greg and me getting closer these past few days? I guess no one is that clueless. No wonder they were gone all day yesterday. It's making so much more sense now.

"We're just thinking about how amazing it's going to be on the slopes today," says Greg, saving me from having to answer.

Making myself some oatmeal, I add brown sugar and cinnamon to it.

"And we'll be right next to you," says Greg, looking at me. "Plus, you're a natural."

My smile grows bigger knowing that he means it. He grins back at me, his eyes a soft, milk chocolate color.

Gwen gives an annoyed grunt and continues eating her oatmeal.

When we make it up to the chairlift, the lines are already packed. Looks like we weren't the only ones who thought skiing was a good idea.

Being back in the same place that was the beginning of the end for Maverick and me makes me feel tense. But seeing how far I've come since then gives me a surge of pride.

As soon as I get going on the slopes, I'm back in my element and feeling great.

Trent and Gwen go down the harder slopes, showing off with some jumps. I think after I've had some practice, I'll be ready to take those on too. I never want to be this rusty again. I should have never let Maverick hold me back from skiing. It's something I've always loved.

Greg sticks to the medium runs with me all morning. It's such a sweet, simple gesture. Even though he could join Gwen and Trent on the more difficult runs, he'd rather spend the time with me.

After a couple hours of skiing, we're all in line at the ski lift. Gwen and I ride up together. Trent and Greg ride up behind us.

"Having fun?" Gwen asks me as the bar comes down over us on our fifth time up the lift.

"Uh, yeah, I'm a natural, remember?"

Gwen and I both laugh.

"I've missed you, Hol," Gwen says, leaning in for a hug. And even though we talk regularly and have been with each other practically every day this trip, I get what she's saying. I wasn't me before. I was a shell of myself.

"I've missed you too," I say, embracing her.

When the ski lift reaches the top of the slope, Gwen eagerly hops off. "Meet you at the bottom," she says before humming the song "Bye Bye" by Jo Dee Messina. Gwen zooms off toward a harder run, waving her ski pole at me. She's fearless. I want to grow up to be her one day.

As I see Trent and Greg come up behind me, I can't help but think how wonderful this vacation has been. Hanging out and chatting with Gwen and the boys is so relaxing. There's something about lifelong friends that makes anyone feel whole.

"Gwennie leave already?" asks Greg, looking around for Gwen.

"Yep. I swear she's trying to break speed records with how fast she flies down these runs."

We laugh and carry on all the way to the front of the line. Greg seems at ease, which is perfect because I don't want him fretting about last night.

I grin as I think about waking up together this morning. My cheeks turn pink at the thought of Gwen and Trent seeing us. Greg's been so patient with me, so understanding about taking things slow and letting me process everything that's happened this week. I can't believe how different my life is now from when I first got here. I've ditched the person who was holding me back and realized I need to focus on me, my own dreams, and my own happiness. I'm quitting my job, changing careers completely, and opening a bakery. And maybe—I look at Greg standing just a few inches from me—maybe I'll have a new person to go on that journey with.

I think about how hard we've laughed, how passionately we've kissed, how wonderful our conversations have been— especially talking each other through the misunderstanding last night. A pang of loss hits me hard as I remember that we have only three days left.

"Who burst your balloon?" Trent asks. "Why are you so sad-looking all of a sudden?"

"Oh, nothing, just thinking how we'll be heading back soon. I'm not ready for our vacation to be over," I reply. I'm not ready to not be spending almost every hour with Greg.

"True," says Trent, "but you're going to be so busy setting up your bakery when we get back that you won't have time to miss the vacation."

"Plus," adds in Greg, "my mom and dad own the cabin, so we can come back anytime."

"I know." I smile at him. We will definitely be coming back here together another time. "This has been nice though."

"Agreed!" says Trent. "Next time we won't wait as long to go on a vacay together!"

"You down for a medium run?" Greg asks Trent. "Or you going to try and beat Gwen to the bottom?"

"I beat her enough times already. I'm down for a medium run," says Trent.

I roll my eyes at Trent's bragging.

Laughing, Greg turns to me. "Ready?" He gestures to a medium run.

I pause, a glint in my eyes and a surge of confidence filling within me.

"I see the wheels spinning. What's up?" Greg asks.

I look around at the groups of people going down different slopes, my eye catching on one of the slope names. "I'm thinking I want to try something different."

"Really?" Greg says.

I nod, a wide smile spreading across my face.

"What do you have in mind?" Greg asks.

I nod my head toward a sign that reads "Nutty as a Fruitcake."

"What!" says Trent, following my gaze. "That's a black diamond level!"

"Are you sure?" Greg asks.

I feel more confident by the minute. I don't know why I let Maverick stop me from skiing so many times. I should never have let that happen. I've waited too long, but not anymore. I'm back now. I'm no longer the Holly that bends to the will of someone else. I'm no longer the Holly that puts everyone else before her. I'm the Holly that embraces herself and knows she's a wonderful skier, that she's always been one. I reach to where I know my lotus necklace sits against my chest; I can't touch it, but just knowing where it is and what it represents gives me an extra boost of confidence.

"Yes, I'm sure," I tell Greg.

"All right!" says Trent, throwing a fist in the air.

"Lead the way," says Greg, smiling at me.

I smile at Greg and with a nod of my head, we take off down the black diamond run side by side.

I fly over the drops, feeling light and happy. This black diamond has quite a few boulders that we have to swerve around, but I take each one smoothly, effortlessly. The steep incline only enhances my sense of achievement. No longer the belittled, timid Holly I was with Maverick, I have found my confidence, and it's invigorating.

When we get to the bottom and over to the lifts, we see Gwen waiting for us.

Gwen laughs. "What took you all so long?"

"Not everyone can be as badass as you, G," I say, laughing.

"True!" Gwen says.

"But you're quite the badass yourself," Trent says, nudging me.

Gwen looks at me confused.

"I just did a black diamond run," I tell her.

"What!" she says, jumping up and down. "You did it, Hol!"

"I did!" I say, beaming. "I'm back."

We spend the next few hours on difficult runs. It's exhilarating and I never want to stop skiing.

Jumping off the ski lift again, I notice the clouds are growing thicker and darker. More people are leaving than joining us on the slopes.

"Better be the last one for us," says Greg, looking at the sky.

"Yep," agrees Trent. "A storm is coming in, for sure."

"Perfect," says Gwen. "Drinking some hot cocoa while the snow swirls outside is all I want to do this afternoon."

"That sounds magical," I agree.

"As long as the cocoa has peppermint, I'm in," Greg says.

"Oh, gross!" says Gwen. "You might as well wring out my toothpaste in your mug."

"What?" I ask Gwen. "You don't like peppermint hot cocoa? What about Greg's world-famous hot cocoa?"

"Oh, absolutely not!" Gwen says.

"Have I ever tried your world-famous hot cocoa?" Trent asks Greg.

Greg shrugs. "If not, I can whip some up for you when we're back at the cabin."

"Nice!" says Trent.

"You're going to love it," I tell Trent.

"When did you try it?" Trent asks me.

Greg and I look at each other, smiles breaking across our faces. Snow flutters to the ground.

"I made some for her the first night we got here," Greg says.

"And it was perfect," I say. Not only because it tasted delicious but because that night changed everything. Who knows how different this week would've looked if Greg hadn't taken that earlier flight and if that snowstorm hadn't delayed Gwen and Trent.

"You two are weird," says Gwen, rolling her eyes. "I don't understand the fascination with peppermint in your hot cocoa. It's like drinking orange juice after you brush your teeth."

We're all laughing as we make our way to our last run.

As we reach midway down the slope, the snowfall picks up. The winter wonderland around us quickly turns into a snowstorm, making it difficult to ski.

Torrents of large snowflakes fall. The wind intensifies, almost toppling us over. By the time we reach the end of the run, a thick wall of snow drapes over the slope, making it hard to see more than twenty feet ahead. I pause a moment, adjusting my ski goggles in hopes that I will see better, but it doesn't help.

"Stay close," Greg yells. I can barely hear him over the gusts of wind. "We'll get to the path and follow it back to the cabin," he continues.

I nod, and we slowly trudge through the quickly accumulating snow on the trail. I hope the forest will give us some sanctuary from the storm.

The wind howls, and the storm dumps waves of snow on us. It's coming down so hard that there's barely any visibility. The storm is not easing up in the slightest, as much as I'd hoped it would.

Gwen walks a foot or so ahead of me. I keep my eyes focused on her bright pink ski suit, trying to stay in line. I know the boys are just ahead of her, but I can no longer see or hear them.

We trudge on for much longer than it should've taken us to reach the cabin. But there's still no relief from the snow squall. The path is wide enough that it acts like a tunnel, whipping us harder with the snow and wind.

Suddenly I lose sight of Gwen. I must've fallen behind a bit. I stop, hoping to catch sight of Gwen's pink ski suit or anyone's ski suit for that matter, but I can't see anything but white flakes falling furiously to the ground.

"Gwen!" I yell, but there's no response. My voice probably isn't strong enough to be heard. "Gwen!" I try again, this time louder.

Nothing.

The wind only gets stronger, the snow coming down harder.

"Trent!"

"Greg!"

Nothing.

No worries, I know the way back. I've walked to the slopes and back so many times it should be like second nature to me, right? I pick up my pace a bit, confident I'll catch back up to the group in no time.

The snow continues to fall in blankets, causing me to have to pick up my feet higher with each step.

Flakes pelt my face, and the wind pulls at my ski suit.

Am I heading in the right direction? If I haven't already missed the turn to the cabin, then it should be coming up soon. If I did already pass the turn, then I should see the open valley where Greg took me to watch the sunrise. I would recognize either place, right?

I stop to get my bearings. Am I heading east or west right now? All I see are trees and snow. I can't tell where I am.

Panicking, I take a deep breath and try to concentrate.

Confidently, I decide to keep walking in the direction I am going. I take a few steps forward, and then my foot catches.

I try to steady myself, but I can't get my footing. And then I'm falling down the mountainside. Pain sears through me as I collide with rocks, snow, and branches. I reach out, trying to grab on to something to slow myself down.

Finally, I catch on to a branch.

My body whips to a sudden stop. I'm jerked backward. My head slams against the trunk of a tree.

A stinging pain rips across the back of my head.

I sit up, gasping. One of my gloves is missing, and my snowsuit is torn, exposing me to the snow. I reach up to touch my head, and when I pull my hand away, it's covered in blood.

Blinking, I feel my head grow heavy. This can't be good.

I try to stand, but I'm hit with excruciating pain that shoots up through my leg. I land back in the snow.

Lovely. So now I'm lost, hurt, and stuck here.

You win, Murphy. I give up.

I shiver as the snow piles into the tear in my snowsuit. What I wouldn't give to be in Greg's arms feeling his soft kisses on my lips, his warm body up against mine.

My head throbs, and I feel dizzy.

And then everything is black.

CHAPTER 28
Greg

I breathe a sigh of relief as the cabin comes into view. I sit at the bottom of the deck, waiting for everyone else to make it back. Only a few flakes flutter to the ground. The only sign a storm has passed through are the added inches of powder and the snowdrifts piled against the trees.

Trent's only a few minutes behind me, the look of relief evident on his face when he realizes he made it.

"That was miserable," he says, walking up the steps and leaning his skis against the side of the house.

"Yeah, it was."

"But it wouldn't be a northern winter if we didn't have a handful of those snow squalls, right? I'm glad it finally eased up."

"As long as everyone makes it back safely, we'll be good to go," I say, scanning the tree line for the girls.

After a few more minutes, Gwen emerges from the path and heads up the steps of the deck.

"Holly behind you?" I ask.

"She should be," Gwen replies.

I nod, and we continue to watch the forest tree line waiting for Holly to emerge.

A few more minutes pass and still nothing.

"How far behind you was she?" I ask Gwen.

"I'm not sure. Close I think."

I pace around the deck.

"Don't worry," says Trent, "I'm sure she'll be here soon."

I don't respond.

Panic builds inside me. I squeeze my eyes shut, my adrenaline spiking. A slight shiver runs through me. "It's been too long," I tell them. "I'm going to look for her."

"Yeah," says Trent, looking as worried as I feel, "it shouldn't have taken her this long."

"You think something's wrong?" Gwen says, alarmed. "Is she okay?"

"I don't know, Gwen," I say. If I stay here another second, I'm going to combust.

"We'll come with you," Gwen says, standing up.

"No," I say. "We shouldn't all go back out there and risk getting lost too."

"He's right," says Trent calmly, putting his hand on Gwen's shoulder. "Greg will find her."

Gwen tries to argue, but one look from me and she steps back, standing with Trent.

"Go get your girl," says Trent. "I'm sure she's turned around is all."

I hand off my skis to Trent and turn swiftly back to the forest path. I have to trust that Trent will keep Gwen at the cabin, no matter how worried she is for Holly.

Within moments, I'm down the forest path and can no longer see the deck. My mind is already a flurry of panic, not knowing where to even begin in my search for Holly.

"Holly!" I call out as I slowly scan back and forth next to the sides of the path.

I look for footsteps, dropped skis, broken branches, any signs that someone has taken the wrong step.

Minutes creep by.

Step by step, my search is painfully slow, but I don't want to miss any sign that Holly might be somewhere.

The panic I've been feeling hits a new high.

Breathe, just breathe. You'll find her. And then I will never let her go again.

"Holly!" I yell again.

She's just lost.

She's completely fine.

She has to be.

I've wasted too many years not being with her. I can't lose her again.

My heart is racing. Fear for her keeps me moving along and searching, screaming her name. Tears threaten to fall from my eyes.

"Holly, where are you?" My voice trembles in my ears. I try to calm my nerves. If I'm panicking, I may miss something. And I can't do that. Holly needs me.

I still, holding my breath. I see something sticking out of the snow. Frantic, I run toward it. It's one of my parents' skis.

"Holly!" I yell out.

She must be close. She has to be.

I hear a faint moan.

I yell again, "I'm here! Where are you, Holly?"

Then, I spot her a few feet away. She's lying in the snow, not moving.

"I'm coming!" I yell, adrenaline coursing through me.

I drop to my hands and knees, crawling to her side.

"Greg?" she asks, her eyes fluttering.

"Yeah, it's me," I say. "You're going to be okay. I found you." She doesn't look to be in good shape, but she's communicating.

I lean my cheek against her, feeling the freezing cold of her forehead.

"Here, wear this," I say, taking off my coat and putting it over the top of her torn ski suit.

I look over her for any signs of harm, checking her pupils. I feel around the back side of her head and neck.

She's bleeding.

My chest tightens. I take a deep breath. *Stay focused, Greg. You need to get her out of this forest.*

"We're going to go back to the cabin now," I tell her, scooping her up in my arms.

She gives me a half-hearted smile. "My leg . . ." she mumbles.

I gently pull her closer to me, trying to warm her the best I can.

She burrows deeper against me, resting her head against my chest, tears falling from her face.

"Shh, it's okay. I'm here now," I tell her.

My love for her is overflowing. I give her a soft kiss on the forehead and walk toward the cabin.

"Greg, I . . ." she says.

And then she goes limp in my arms.

"Holly!"

She doesn't respond.

What's happening to her? Why isn't she coming to? My stomach tightens and a lump of worry forms in my throat. I don't know what will happen after this trip, but one thing is for sure: I will not lose Holly.

She's my heart.

My everything.

I pull Holly against me and trudge quickly through the snow.

Knowing the path like the back of my hand, I return to the cabin without much incident. Gwen and Trent are pacing by the back door. The second we come into view, they rush out of the house.

"Get the snowmobile, now!" I tell Trent. "The keys are on the hook by the garage door."

Trent takes one look at Holly and runs back inside.

Gwen's eyes widen when she takes in the sight of us. "Oh my gosh!" she says. "What happened?"

"Not now," I say curtly.

"Is she okay?" Gwen says. "Where did you find her? Is that blood? Where is it coming from? Is she breathing?"

"I said not now," I snap at her and then instantly soften. "Gwennie, I need you to focus, okay?"

She wipes a tear from her face.

"We're going to take her to the ER and figure this out," I tell her.

Trent pulls up behind me with the snowmobile.

"Can you drive them?" Trent asks Gwen.

She nods.

"Good," he says, stepping off the snowmobile. "I know Holly will want you at the hospital. And here," Trent adds as he takes his coat and drapes it over Holly, "just in case."

Barely room for the three of us, I manage to sit behind Gwen with Holly still in my arms. As we drive down the snowy roads, I look down at Holly.

She's still and pale.

"Come back to me," I whisper.

CHAPTER 29
Holly

I open my eyes, blinking at a harsh light overhead. My head is pulsating, and I try to sit up.

"Woah there," says a nurse in scrubs. "Just lie back down, hon." I do as she says without any argument.

"You're at the hospital in Snowden," she tells me. "You've been in an accident, but you're okay now."

An accident? What happened? We were skiing, and then we decided to head back to the cabin. I remember that much for sure. But the rest is a little fuzzy. I know there was a storm, and I think I lost the group. But how did I get hurt?

"You have a nasty cut on the back of your head," says the nurse, "and your leg is beaten up, but we're going to take good care of you."

A cut on the back of my head? My leg? And just at the mention of the injuries, a wave of pain surges through me. I remember falling down the mountain and hitting my head. No wonder it hurt to sit up.

But how did I get back here?

"Your friends will be relieved you're up," she says.

My friends are here? Greg, I remember Greg finding me. He must have been so worried. Did he carry me all the way back? And Gwen and Trent, are they okay?

After the nurse stitches me up and I've taken some X-rays, she leads me to a private room.

"You rest right here," the nurse says. "I'm going to go grab the doctor. He wanted to talk to you once you woke up."

I lie down in the bed and feel completely exhausted. I try to rest but my body throbs.

Moments later, an older man with a grandfatherly demeanor walks in. "Ms. Palmer, I'm Dr. Carter. How are you feeling?"

"It's Holly, and not too great," I say.

"Let me take a look at that leg, and then we'll look over your X-ray."

He adjusts the blanket off my leg. I've got some nasty bruising around my ankle and lower leg, and the ankle is swollen to practically double the size. The sight makes me queasy; this can't be good. He presses various places on my leg, and even though I can tell he is trying to be gentle, pain sears through me, and I grip the blankets.

Content with what he sees, he takes some images out of a folder and puts them on the light-up frame on the wall. After seeing my leg, I don't want to see the X-rays, but I have to know. My eyes follow his hands as he adjusts the images on the frame.

"Well, Holly, it appears you've broken your leg and have a concussion."

"That explains me blacking out," I mumble.

He nods then continues, "Thankfully you won't need surgery for your broken leg, but we will need to get you a cast. Right now, your leg is too swollen to put one on, so you'll be staying with us for a bit until the swelling goes down. And it will be good for us to monitor your concussion too. Until then, I'm going to have the nurse give you something stronger for the pain to help you sleep through the night. I'll be back in the morning to check in on you."

"Thank you." I say meekly, relieved that I'll be getting some medication to ease the pain. I should be grateful I don't need surgery, but all I want to do is go back to the cabin and curl up with Greg.

The doctor takes the X-rays and exits the room. A few moments later, the nurse comes in with pain pills.

"Are you feeling up to some visitors, hon? You have two very anxious friends in the waiting room."

"Yes," I say, "it would be great to see some familiar faces."

Minutes later, Gwen bursts into my room. "Holly!" she says, a look of relief on her face. Greg walks in behind her. Gwen wraps her arms around me, and I wince.

"Sorry," she says, backing away.

"It's okay," I say, giving her a weak smile.

Gwen looks over at Greg, concern etched on her face. She pulls up a chair next to my bed, looking me over.

"What happened?" she asks.

Greg walks over to the windows, silently looking outside. Even so solemn, he looks handsome.

"Greg said he found you knocked out cold in the snow." Gwen grabs my hand. "I was so worried," she says, eyes filling with tears.

"Hey," I say, lightly squeezing her fingers, "I'm okay now."

She smiles and wipes a tear from her cheek.

"I don't remember much," I say, "only that shortly after we got on the trail and into the forest line, I lost you all. I tried calling for you. But with the way the wind was, I could barely hear myself."

Greg shifts to face us. His brow is furrowed, and he looks sad. "I kept going in the direction I thought the cabin was. I remember seeing what I thought was the turn, but I was mistaken and then I tripped. I remember falling and then nothing really after that."

I look over at Greg, and he looks at the floor. "I vaguely remember Greg finding me."

"Yeah, he did," says Gwen. "He carried you back to the cabin, and then he and I drove you here on the snowmobile."

"Thank you, Greg," I say, looking at him again.

He nods but doesn't look at me.

"What did the doctor say?" Gwen asks.

"I have a broken leg and a concussion. They're going to keep me here a bit just to keep an eye on things."

"I'm so sorry, Hol," says Gwen. "Anything we can do for you?"

"No," I say, shaking my head, "just waiting for the pain medication to kick in."

Greg paces back and forth by the window. He looks tense.

"Actually, G," I say, "could you run back to the cabin and get me some clothes? I'm not sure where mine ended up."

"Of course," says Gwen, standing up. "I'll call Margot back to give her an update. I called her while we were waiting, and she made me promise to call her back as soon as I knew something. I'll be back in a few. And you're not going to want your old clothes back."

As soon as Gwen leaves, I turn to Greg. "Sit," I say, glancing at the seat Gwen just vacated.

He sits and immediately rubs the back of his neck, avoiding eye contact with me.

"Don't do that," I say softly, reaching out my hand for his.

"Don't rub my neck?" he asks, wrapping his fingers around mine.

"No, I mean, don't beat yourself up. I know what you're thinking. You're blaming yourself for everything that happened, but it isn't your fault."

"Well, it's not your fault either. I wouldn't be able to forgive myself if something truly bad happened to you, Holly."

He gives a shuttered breath and gently rubs his thumb back and forth over the top of my hand.

"Seeing you that way, I just couldn't. . . . My mind kept going to dark places. I said I would care for you, protect you. I didn't do that, and it's my fault for not watching the sky and for not walking with you back to the cabin."

"Greg, don't. Please, it was a freak storm, and it would have been near impossible for us to walk hand in hand. I know you are trying to take care of me. It's why you found me so quickly after I got hurt. It's why you pushed me out of the way back at the Sounds game when we were kids. Let's just blame Murphy," I say, squeezing his hand playfully.

Letting out a huff, he says, "I don't know what it is with you and Murphy's Law. I'll never understand why you always think he's out to get you." He looks over at me laying in the bed, his thumb lightly tracing circles on the back of my hand. "But this time, okay, we can blame Murphy."

The tension easing from his shoulders, he leans over and kisses my forehead gently.

"I'm just going to rest for a bit until Gwen gets back," I say groggily as the medicine works itself into me. Greg nods.

Before I drift into sleep, my thoughts keep going back to Greg. To our time together at the cabin. To when we were kids, then teenagers heading off in different directions for college.

To when he saved me from the baseball at the Sounds game—the ball that I still have at home sitting on my bookshelf. The ball I kept to remind me of our friendship but now realize meant more than that. This whole time, the ball has been a symbol of my feelings for Greg. Even as a kid, my subconscious knew that Greg would always be there for me. How am I just realizing that I've had feelings for him since childhood?

And then I'm whisked back to more memories. Greg being there for me and letting me cry on his shoulder when I found out Maverick cheated on me. Greg eating all my crazy baking creations as a kid, even the ones that no one should have ever had to endure. Teaching me how to ski the many times we came to the cabin growing up. Helping me up when I fell in the snow the day I'd gotten here. Making sure I was warm and had a place to sleep away from Trent's snoring. Making snow angels with me, laughing with me, helping me develop For the Love of Sugar. And most of all, giving me the confidence to be myself these past few days in Snowden. On and on, the memories flood my mind until one point is clear as day throughout all the memories.

No matter the age, no matter the situation, whenever Greg has looked at me, there has always been something in his eyes. Like he was memorizing my face, my expressions, my whole being. He was seeing me for me. The real me.

He's always looked at me like I'm the most amazing thing in his life.

It hits me like a brick. Greg's been in love with me for years. I know Trent implied that when we talked, but it's all finally clicking.

My thoughts keep going back to Greg. He makes me feel safe. He makes me feel beautiful and wanted. Like I'm the best thing in his world. He loves my baking. He's never been demanding or cruel. He makes me laugh. He builds me up. And dang, can he kiss.

Oh.

My.

Gosh.

Oh my gosh. . . .

I'm in love with Greg.

I don't know when it happened or what the turning point was for me. But I'm one hundred percent head over heels in love with that man.

CHAPTER 30
Greg

Holly is going to be okay. Relief floods through me. She doesn't blame me for getting hurt. Instead, my beautiful Holly was worried about me. She tried to take care of me, when she is the one in the hospital.

Love courses through my veins as I look at this incredible woman lying in a hospital bed. When she gets out of this place, I am going to tend to her every need. She will want for nothing. I didn't think I could love her more than I had before, but somehow, seeing her safe in this hospital bed, my love has grown. I will spend every day showing her how much she means to me. How much she's loved and appreciated.

There's a light knock at the door, and Gwen slips in with some fresh clothes and hot cocoas.

"She's asleep," I say, nodding toward Holly.

"Good," Gwen says, handing me a cup of cocoa and placing one for Holly on a side table. Then she wraps me in a giant hug, and I almost spill my drink.

"What's this for?" I ask Gwen.

She sighs, sitting down in the chair next to mine. "For rescuing my best friend. I can't even imagine what it must have felt like to find her like that."

"Relief at finding her, followed by pure panic when she went limp in my arms."

Gwen places her hand on my arm. "You're a good guy, Greg."

"You ever doubt that?" I ask, trying to lighten the mood.

"Nope, just letting you know in case you forgot," she teases back.

"Gwennie, I thought I'd lost her. I can't lose her. I am head over heels, truly and deeply in love with Holly."

"I know," says Gwen.

"You do?"

"Yeah, it's pretty obvious you'd do anything for her. I saw the way you lit up, pure joy on your face every time she stepped into the room. The change in your demeanor, the openness she brought out of you. Around her, you are happier, carefree, no longer seemingly burdened with the weight of the world. A sister wants such happiness for her brother. Then I saw the pain on your face when she didn't come out of the woods after us. The fear in your eyes when you carried her back to the cabin. Anyone who feels that strongly for my friend deserves the happiness I know you two will have."

"Thank you. That means a lot. You're a great little sis, you know?"

"Of course," she says, chuckling to herself. "I mean, it's me. What did you expect?"

Time blurs by at the hospital. Gwen, Trent, and I alternate staying with Holly and running to the cabin. It kills me to see Holly in pain, but eventually the swelling in her leg goes down enough for a cast, and the doctors are no longer worried about negative side effects from her concussion. Soon Holly is sleeping less and complaining of boredom more. And then she's discharged, and Holly and I are on our way back to the cabin to meet Trent and Gwen.

When we pull the snowmobile into the driveway, it's late. The stars are twinkling like Christmas lights against the dark blue of the sky.

"Home." Holly breathes out a sigh, joy sparkling in her eyes like the stars. "I know I've only been away for two days, but it feels like forever."

I nod in agreement. "It does."

"And the fact that you are here with me," she pauses, smiling up at me, "is just the icing on top."

Gwen and Trent greet us at the door and hold it open for us.

"We have the fire going in the den," says Trent.

"We're going to go make some tacos for a late dinner," says Gwen. "We didn't want to eat without you since we knew you'd be coming home tonight."

"That sounds delicious," Holly says. "Thank you."

Trent and Gwen head into the kitchen, and Holly moves farther into the living room.

It takes her a bit longer to walk across to the couches in front of the fireplace, but she insists she can do it without my help. I take a few breaths with my eyes closed to steady my beating heart. She will be fine. The doctor said she'd be as good as new within a few months.

I take her in as she sits in front of the crackling fireplace. It makes her skin glow from the warmth. Her messy bun is coming undone after the slow snowmobile ride back to the cabin. She is beautiful, gorgeous in my eyes. I am full of an intense love for this strong woman.

My heart swells with emotion seeing her here back at the cabin. Just a couple days ago, I'd thought I lost her forever. The lotus necklace on her chest shines in the light of the fire. What a perfect symbol of this woman who is so strong and pure.

Holly shifts in her seat, winces, and then gives me a smile.

"How are you feeling?" I say.

"I've been better," she replies, "but honestly I'm happy to be back here with you."

We smile at each other for a minute, my cheeks growing warm. I look around the cabin, and my thoughts flicker to the moments we've shared. Holly dripping wet from falling in the snow. Our hands touching on her mug. Cooking, baking, playing games. Making snow angels. Kissing. Falling asleep together just three nights before.

I'd always felt comfortable at my family's cabin, but now it holds an even more special place in my heart. This is where Holly and I found each other. Where we overcame obstacles, found new beginnings, and decided to take a chance on each other.

I sit on the couch next to her, looking at the crackling fire. "Holly, I have something to tell you. I've been wanting to tell you for, well for forever, honestly." I break off, running my hand over my face in frustration.

"It's okay, Greg," Holly says gently, smiling up at me as she places a hand on my leg.

"No, it's not okay. I've been trying to tell you for days. It never seems like the right time, with you at the hospital, or I just get too nervous." I sigh. I can do this. I have to tell her. She means everything to me and thinking I'd lost her while carrying her limp body to the cabin almost broke me. I can't waste any more time. No more excuses.

She reaches her hand out to me.

I turn to face Holly, taking her hand in mine. A familiar spark ignites in me, and I stare at her, amazed at how I feel once again at this simple touch. The same spark I'd felt when we'd first held hands at the Sounds game almost thirteen years ago. The same spark I felt when our hands touched reaching for Holly's mug our first night here.

"What I want to say is . . ."

"Greg, I know," she says, wrapping both of my hands in hers.

But I can't stop here. There's so much I want to express to her.

"It's, well, Holly, this may freak you out. I mean, I hope it doesn't, but I'm just going to say it."

I take a deep breath.

"Greg, I know," she says again softly, calmly.

But I continue on. I've had these words and feelings for years, and I need to get them out.

"Ever since we were kids and you walked into my home, I've had feelings for you. Before that, I'd never believed in love at first sight, but you took my breath away. You took the key to my heart the moment you first smiled at me. I moved out of state because I couldn't bear seeing you with someone else. It broke me. I was eager to come on this trip because I knew I'd get to see you. At the time, I didn't think anything could possibly happen between us, but I just wanted to be near you again. I tried to keep my feelings at bay, but I couldn't help the chemistry that was building between us. My feelings for you just kept growing stronger with each passing glance, laugh, every moment with you."

I squeeze her hand gently.

Taking a deep breath, I lock eyes with her. "Holly, I . . ." My voice breaks. So much emotion pools within me. Her eyes glisten in the light from the fire. It shatters the last reservations I have inside. "I love you, Holly. I've loved you for thirteen years."

Tears in her eyes, she whispers, "I know. That's what I've been trying to tell you." And then she says the words I've been longing to hear for half my life: "I love you too, Greg."

I still for a moment, my brain trying to figure out if she'd said what I think she said. My eyes grow wide, a huge grin lighting up my entire face.

"You what?" I ask softly.

"I love you," she says again. She wipes the tears from her eyes, smiling as she reaches for my face. I lean in slowly. When we are a breath away, she looks me straight in the eyes.

"Greg, this past week, you've shown me a love I've never had from anyone. I can't even put into words how much I love you."

With my heart bursting with joy, I feel her press her lips hard against mine, kissing me as tears fall from her eyes. I kiss her back softly but fiercely. Her proclamation of love stirs something within me, and I hope it has in her too.

"I've been waiting to hear those words for thirteen years," I say, leaning her back against the couch. I tilt her face gently up, and I kiss her with all the love inside me. I treasure this moment. Soft kisses, so different from the heated kisses we'd shared. Our tongues dance a slow waltz. These kisses are like promises. Promises that we will be there for each other—be what each other needs. I kiss her lips, her cheeks, and then her forehead, relishing the fact that we both finally feel the same way about each other.

We pull apart, and I gently stroke her cheek with my thumb. I'm smiling so wide my face might split in two, but I can't stop. "Will you be my girlfriend, Holly?"

Her eyes light up as her smile grows to encompass her whole being.

"Yes. That would make me beyond happy." She squeezes my hand, leaning into my touch.

I lean over, kissing her gently again.

Holly loves me.

ONE YEAR
Later . . . .

EPILOGUE
Holly

"Hol, we have another event I need to book you in March," says Gwen, walking through the bakery like she owns the place.

For The Love of Sugar opened last May and we've been busy ever since. Gwen hadn't been lying. Her clients are always in need of a baker. The catering side of my business got me up and going, but when word got out that I'd opened my own shop, customers poured in daily for goodies. Not to mention putting in orders for birthdays, anniversaries, work parties, and so many other events.

Chessie Valley was the perfect place for Greg and my relationship to grow. After we left the cabin last year, he went back to New York for just enough time to get things taken care of at his condo and put in his notice at work. The marina's business has been booming since he took over its marketing and website. We've never been happier and are nearly inseparable.

"What's the name, and I'll add it to my calendar," I tell Gwen.

"The Johnson and Kelley family reunion, and then hurry up, we're supposed to be catching our flight soon."

"I'm coming," I say, scribbling down the name.

"We don't want to chance getting caught in another storm that could keep us away from the cabin," she laughs, referring to what happened to her last year.

"We won't," I tell her. "I checked the weather, and it's supposed to be crystal blue skies, no chance for any snowstorms."

"I can't wait to have some girl time—just the two of us," Gwen says. "You and Greg have been inseparable the past year, and as much as that makes me happy, I want you all to myself for a bit."

Gwen and I reach the airport right on time. On our flight, there's an extra seat in our row, so we celebrate our luck and stretch out. At the rental car agency, we end up getting an upgrade because the car we wanted wasn't returned in time. How great is that!

"I'm actually excited to be coming back," I tell Gwen as we drive toward the Snowden lodge.

"Same, girl." She smiles at me.

Without a snowstorm, we make record time, and soon we're skiing at the slopes.

The weather is a perfect, bright blue sky with barely any clouds. I smile, breathing in the fresh mountain air. Looking down at my leg, I move it around. It'd taken a few months to get back to normal, but now it's better than ever.

"Okay, which run do we want to try first?" Gwen asks.

"You know which one," I say, nodding toward the "Nutty as a Fruitcake" sign.

"I should've known that once you got back into skiing, you'd never come off those black diamond runs."

I laugh and push off with my skis. I had stuck to what I'd said. I kept up with skiing. Greg and I took many weekend trips up to Snowden once my leg was better. I love skiing with the feel of the wind whipping through my hair. Though I do love a nice, leisurely medium run, the black diamond runs are exhilarating.

"Nutty as a Fruitcake" is my favorite. It has a great mix of steep slopes, small jumps, and short drop-offs that let me flex my skiing abilities. I take a small jump, and while I'm in the air, I feel like I can do anything. I land with ease, even spraying a little snow as I zigzag down the mountain.

After a short drop-off, I know I'm nearing the end of the run. Gwen is nowhere in sight. As is typical for her, she probably took a straight shot down to the bottom.

Rounding one of the last corners, I notice something near the end of the run. Curiosity has the better of me, but I can't quite tell what it is.

Passing the last line of trees and getting closer, I gasp after seeing Greg. What is he doing here? But I don't care why he's here. I'm just so happy that he is.

And then I notice what's behind him. My heart stops, and seconds later it begins to beat frantically. Made with a bunch of skis are the words "Marry Me?"

I slow my skis as I approach, stopping right in front of him. We lock eyes, and he smiles, dropping to one knee.

"Greg?" I ask timidly.

He grins, lifting up a baseball-helmet bucket packed with snow and holding something glistening in the middle of it.

"Holly," he says, "you captured my heart the very first time I met you. My soul aches to be with you when I'm not. Our time together this past year has been nothing short of magical. I love being with you, so now I'm asking to be with you for eternity. It would make me the happiest man in the world if you would agree to be my wife."

I stare at him, and my breath catches in my chest, tears leaking out of my eyes. I'm stunned into silence, but Greg just smiles easily at me with so much love in his eyes.

I nod, and finally able to formulate the words, I say, "Yes, Greg, I'd love to marry you!"

He reaches for my hand, pulls my glove off gently, and picks the most beautiful diamond ring from the snow nestled in the helmet. He places it on my finger before standing to pull me into a hug and then kissing me fiercely.

Breaking away to look at Greg, I smile. Nothing could ever make me feel happier than I am at this moment. I have everything I've ever wanted and a guy who means everything to me. This is what pure joy feels like. I truly am the luckiest woman in the world.

Take that, Murphy!

The End

JESS JEFFERIES

Jess currently lives in Tennessee with her husband, three kids, and their dog. She has a bubbly personality and can almost always be found with a smile on her face.

While reading has always been a passion of hers, she has also dabbled in writing short stories and poems since she was a little girl. *Thirteen-Year Crush* is her debut novel, a romcom.

When Jess is not writing, you can find Jess swimming with her kids, playing board games, or snuggled up with a book and a comfy blanket.

Follow her on Instagram and TikTok:
@jessjefferieswrites

www.jessjefferieswrites.com